Lads Reunited

Max Speed

Supported by 50mph books

"What is it?" I asked. I was surrounded by books and he was passing me another.

For you

This was really his book. I jumped into the first page.

1

Each day starts with disappointment and then gets worse. Today was different – it deteriorated quicker.

Light. Piercing. Nose moving in one direction. Lips in another. Squirming to avoid the glare. Eyelids attacked. Vision screwed up like bottle tops. Slowly untwisting. Burrowing deep into pillow. Sensed the bed board shuffle as she rammed her heaving back against it. The bed cried out in pain. Sound of a book page delicately tugged. Light invading my darkness. Mouth dry. Stuck against the pillow. Waking slowly but still thinking without pronouns. Having two hundred and forty worth of lux staring down is no luxury, especially when energy saving and boxed as warm white. Sounds of tea being sipped. No, slurped. Her cold, cold, cold feet against my legs.

"Fucks sake," I barely muttered. "Point light back." I stumbled my words. "Stop sucking up your tea so loudly......sound mud like."

"It's Darjeeling," she said serrating her sips, slurps, sucks.

I was about to reply, "It's still mud (or tea) when she started.

"*Tom,*" she coughed expelling more than an innocent frog from her throat. "*Tom gl nc d behin im saw m n comin   of gr n cage, head ng his way Tom wa k d fast r. There was no do t the   was aft r h m.*"

I only caught some of the words, some of the sounds but each was scratching.

Light had won. My eyes were defeated. Sleep was ending the nocturnal empire.

"Jesus Sophie, can you not read to yourself?"

"I AM reading to ME," defining her own self within her own sentence......and then hissing like a deflating ball.

"Yeah, but like....not aloud. Read like anyone normal does."

"I want to read like this. I always have. Always will. I was like this when we got married."

"Gods sake Soph," raising my head slightly. "I don't remember you banging out garbled paragraphs of Chinua's '*Things Fall Apart*' as you dazzled slouchingly down the aisle" - in all honesty, I'd just thought of saying that and hadn't muttered a word of it.

I know her capabilities. Her book isn't a paperback.

She's a fury; mythology will one day suggest that she was sprung from mutilated blood......probably. Unceasing in anger. She once tried to throw my clothes out of the window - I was wearing them at the time.

I mumbled the much more slowly awakening, dull: "People must sit away from you on the train."

Barking back, "I'm not on a train. I'm in a bed. And the headphones are in the box of tech we never use anymore."

Oh yes, the crate of appliances that are no use in this modern age (or were no use when we got them in the first place): a juicer, two answering machines, a portable DVD player, a musical popcorn maker, a pair of *wii nunchuk* controllers and a chocolate fountain fondue – the fountain worked but she needed a leisure centre wave machine and some waterpark flumes doused in cocoa to feed that appetite. Even the *George Foreman lean, mean, fat reducing grilling machine* gets turned on more times than me and that's also in the *cupboard under the stairs* – small and dusty with lots of spiders in dark places......but I married her. I can't shove her reading light into that old gadget box so I just reply:

"It's monotonal. Lifeless dictation.....plus I've got the brightest fucking torch injecting me."

Immediately her book tilted to one side. "Ohhhh, I bet you'd like that." **She interrupted herself**, "Anyway, I thought you'd want to be woken." There was silence. Her head hung over me; a predator waiting for her prey to speak. "I repeat. I thought you'd want to be woken."

"Why   would I   need   to   be   woken?" each word pausing to think.

"I'll tell you. Let me just read one more line – *Tom ha.....*" Her words were noticeable, purposeful and clear though slower than before. I still missed most of what she was saying – call it habit (or self-preservation). "*.....wasn't quite sure   but   almost*". She thrust the book towards my face. My head retreated to being half buried within the duvet – the pages hiding the persistent glare from the light.

"I thought *the untalented Mr You* would want to be in a hurry and get out."

I scratched my head. I was unsure. It raised at a slight, acute angle with a gaping thinking hole of a mouth partially dribbling; one eye lid batting away the light. My body remained without movement, a sack of rooted vegetables from the neck down.

She enjoyed the pause. My blank expression. A clean canvas. Vast space of fearful soft nervous tissue. Unable to remember. Unable to even stop the corner of my mouth lactating.

"Isn't it the uni reunion?" Darkness stirred. "Isn't it the university reunion?" Light began creeping through. She poked me in the side. "The uni reunion.....isn't it?" Turning her head and repeating again with such calm, "Reunion.....uni.....is it not?"

SILENCE. My eye lid initially flickered. Remembering I had two eye lids, the second one copied, flickering faster. My neck reached out towards the glow. Her colossal being shadowed me - she was now eager to sit up anticipating my response.

"Not uni reunion is it? Then?" Her words punched me.

"Fuck me!" I shot up like my cock used to when I sat behind a Korean girl called Ji-young in French lessons, in school. I was just 15. She was just 16. She had big breasts. She used to wear a white shirt. We all did but you could see through her top, and needless to say, I went from a predicted A in French to a resultant C just because of her Double D. I mean, 15, and I got an erection staring at her bra strap on her back – nearly 33 years later and my wife could be injecting soap on a rope inside her naked body (she never has by the way) in a bath of bubbles, fully made up, red lips, hair done all 'nice' and even wearing high heels and stockings (not that she does or would in a bath of course) and I'd hardly get it past the horizontal.

Oh, and do me a favour, forget the Ji-young thing if you don't mind. I got drunk in week one at uni, told Baz 'for a laugh'. He told everyone and they all called me Woody Allen until some bloke called Toni on a term long foreign exchange from Turin got his Italian tiddler stuck on the dancefloor during the *YMCA* and everyone forgot about me and started calling him Zippy.

2

 University Reunion

Heart banging. Slow it. Calm down. They won't go without you. Put the pillow back straight. Shave. Shower. Or. Shower. Shave. Get her on side. I need a lift there now.

"A cup of tea Soph?" putting my left sock on.

She paused, recognising the bartering tradition within the relationship. "Ummm," she held eye contact with page 2 of her book. "Lift?" she asked and then glanced up viper-like.

"FabYeahthanksGreatdoyoumindCheers." I waited just one second before looking towards her but it felt like a marriage.

She pursed her lips together tightly. She does that in such a way that I am never totally sure if I'm looking at her face or if she's suddenly turned herself upside down.

"I will give you a lift but just stand there for a moment."

"What?!?"

She placed '*The Talented Mr Ripley*' book on the bedside table and proceeded to pretend to read aloud from an imaginary book, even putting her hands together holding the invisible novel. Nettlesome.

"*It was a bright, cold day in June and the alarm clocks were not striking,*" she giggled.

Genius – Eric Arthur Blair.

Genome deficiency – Sophie.

She mimed the closing of a book.

I imagined the suffocating a pillow could do.

George's words resonated within me. Me, my chin longing to be nuzzled into her breasts, escaping her bad wind under the duvet - I knew I had to be quick to prevent my gritty friends leaving without me in a swirl of dust.

My big brother, Phil, who works on an animal farm, makes such better decisions with femme fatales. For Phil, all relationships are equal. I call him 'Phil Pigeon' - he always manages to get home using the earth's magnetic field. In contrast, I tumble into Trafalgar Square and take up home on the fourth plinth with my Hannibal Lecter; and she has an appetite for both torture and tiramisu.

"You must have had that alarm clock since *1984*," she snorted loudly (from within a cage of rats in room 102 – she always goes one better), liquid escaping from all of her facial caverns.

It was true.

My deceiving traitor of an alarm clock has been going off for 27 reliable years, unfaltering, consistent, honest, true, faithful. That alarm clock has loved me for 27 'effin years non-stop; like clockwork but not clockwork as it's battery operated. One AA – just one single battery and yet today, the day I've been waiting months for, a reunion over 27 years on, on from a time when it was:

go to sleep when you want,

sleep in till when you want,

sleep where you want,

sleep with who you want

(and sometimes <u>not</u> who you want but you've had one drink too many, she's had two too many and it felt like a good idea at 2am and she's offered you toast and a cup of tea, only to wake up to what looks like one of the chimps out of a *PG Tips* advert; only she's hairier, heavier, fatter and with the whitest blotchiest skin. I can't resist anything (including temptation) – the truncated IQ of this toast offering chimp is hardly a paradox but you take what you can get when you're young (though the buttered bread was a little stale the next morning).

It might have been **WHAM!** Bam thank you mam but George Michael's '*Careless Whisper*' was not my song of choice as her lights went on quicker than her tights had come off. More like that lesser known Wham tune: '*Nothing looks the same in the light*'.

Five am and the long goodbye – not as sharp as I wanted the evacuation to be. Neither of us look as good as we did 180 minutes earlier. She can't have put on that much weight lying on her back for 5 minutes and snoring on her side for 175.

I left her hirsute lap in the cover of murkiness wondering if when she was born her parents had bought her a cot or a cage.

Hoping none of my mates would spot me doing the Great Escape (without the motorbike and with less barbed wire) but one 'mate' did, hawking like an officer from a German **POW** camp high in his lookout hostel accommodation. Lee, originally from *Llakcuf*, a village in the Valleys, a decent looking bloke but he always declined the T's: toast, tea and tits in favour of being night watchman. Wales'

13

version of Daffyd Attenborough with his infra-red camera looking out for those escaping from the adjacent female hostel before dawn. An accommodation block now dry but just a few hours earlier dripping with excited moisture, kettles boiling and juices flowing. Thank Christ (and the parents of Mark Zuckerberg) there was no Facebook back then.

I'd side stepped into the shower remembering to remove the 'left' sock still attached to my left foot. Reaching out for a towel and then dropping it in haste by the door stirred the towel police.

"I hope <u>you</u> are using <u>your</u> towel," she managed to cry out, seven significant words of insignificance sandwiched between the read-aloud lines of her book – a book I've read twice before and enjoyed twice before but hearing her paused podcast will mean I'll never ever consider fingering those pages again.

"YOUR towel," she reiterated.

My hand was about to hit the shower button......
beep beep   beep beep   beep beep   beep beep.

"Your ALARM", she said both annoyingly and
annoyed. I ignored the option of asking her to turn it off.
She turns me off nightly. No mans land. I'd get machine
gunned down by her stubborn refusal to switch off the
alarm, no matter how much I pleaded. I decided to hop
naked from the shower, bound across the bedroom and go
over the top of the mattress (and the unflinching 'reader') to
flick it off. My athletic prowess in silencing the beeping
alarm went unnoticed by the unsilenceable 'beeping' reader
and I returned at speed to the shower, refraining from
placing the right sock on my right foot which had distracted
my journey en route. Finally, ready for a shower, I looked
towards a stream of consciousness as the water cascaded
upon me.

That girl from the corner shop. Flirts. Must be half
my age. Probably does it with everyone? Looks good
though scanning the barcode on a six pack of lagers.

And there's the Spanish secretary, Nunca from work – she's like a corner shop herself. Always open. She's invited me round more times than she's baked her own muff pie but I'd just have been one of a long line of cyclists that have ridden her *TourDeFrance*.....and it would have been a mountain stage climb with those thighs.

Never strayed. Always faithful. I enjoy self-harm. I don't even look at other women – Sophie's put me right off. Never considered divorce either. Homicide yes....but not divorce. A few offers over the years. Liquorice females. Tasty and all sorts. Some even handed it on a plate. With a dessert. But I'm destined to live as a sex starved monk – without the silence vow. Noisy cow. I can still hear her reading aloud now. I do love her. Honestly, I do. Don't I? The antonym of Sandra Dee from Grease – won't have sex in bed when she's legally wed. REUNION. Shit. Get washed. Quick. Baz says it's not really a reunion. It's a road trip. It's lads reunited but whichever, I'm getting away.

Is Baz going to look ok after more treatment? Shampoo. *Head and Shoulders. Grecian 2000* soon. Do shops still sell *Grecian 2000*? I saw *Just for Men* in

16

supermarket yesterday. Viagra sold in chemists now. No prescription. Won't need it....check it's still there. Yep. Quick wash just in case - you never know. Never gets properly used. Balls – this shower's gone cold. No sex for me. Even Santa comes once a year. Just Say No. I remember that *Grange Hill 'Just Say No'* song. Been with her 27 years. Why ever did I harpoon her all those years ago. She gave up sex for lent once. Her lent lasts 40 months. I do love her. Don't I? Yeah. But she's like threadworm. You grow to love that. Shit. Stop thinking. Get washed. Get out.

There was a sudden strike at the door; and I was notified of imminent nuclear attack:

"Four minute warning. Four minutes and we're going. Hurry up."

I started wondering if I could be bothered to go to this reunion thing. Pausing as the shower slowed to OFF, I remembered my current position:

Year 27 of the hostage situation

– Yes, the reunion will do me good I thought.

DEODORANT. SHAVE. HAIR GELLED. NASAL HAIR PLUCKED. Body polish in and out – the Eastern Europeans take more care with my car than I do with my ageing chassis. TROUSERS ON. SHIRT ON. TROUSERS OFF. PANTS ON. TROUSERS BACK ON.

"Can I ask you a question?" Sophie said.

"You just have."

"Do you think I should do the no carbs diet or the low carbs diet?"

The most honest answer would have been 'eat as many carbs as you want, just cut down on the doughnuts. Having one in each hand does not mean it's a balanced diet. Oh, and start using the running machine which is upright, clogging up the spare room'. The honest answer would have meant I would be running to meet the lads, only pausing half-way to buy myself a doughnut from *Tesco Express.* Instead I adapted my answer:

"Do the low carbs one. You need carbohydrates but stick to the diet this time". Sophie's diets were similar to the sales in *DFS sofas* – they always end on a Tuesday.

She says that she stops her dieting as I don't support her enough. I do support her. I try to eat half her chocolates. She tells herself that she eats healthily but her *five-a-day* includes *chocolate orange, cherry cola* and a raspberry ripple. Hardly healthy is it? Fruit cake.

SHIRT ON. CLEAN TEETH.

"You should throw that alarm clock away," Sophie said odiously dangling the car keys in the same way that royalty waves.

"Yeah I should." Ensuring I do not disagree with my taxidermist come taxi driver.

"You say that but you never do," Sophie said looking alarmed by the front door, wearing the same pyjamas she was in last night, last week, last month. I don't notice. The woman in white. They match her skin. Pale and baggy.

BAG ON SHOULDERS. SHOES ON. DOOR
OPENED. SOPHIE GUIDED OUT.

"I said you say that but you never do."

DOOR LOCKED. BAG IN BOOT.

Ready but late. She bundled herself into the car.

"I said you say that b—"

"I know. I know. But I never do. I'll tell you what
Soph, when I get bac—"

"If you do," she interjected with perfect timing.

"I'll get a shovel and I'll dig up the garden and I'll
dig a hole and then I'll chuck the alarm clock in it and then
maybe you'd like me to dig another hole and jump in it myself and th—"

She put her hand up. "Shall I start the car?

I nodded.

CAR STARTED.

3

 University Reunion

 Road Trip

Incoming call. Number not known.

"Hello." The same hesitant response I give when expecting an automated 'We believe you've been involved in an accident' call. Don't you just hate those perfidious rings. I haven't had an accident. I say 'no, I've not had an accident' and *Metal Mickey* starts telling me I have. Or I 'politely' tell them to go away and they punish me by dialling back at 3am, 4am, 5am, 6am, 7am but not on a day when my alarm clocks fails, oh no. No customer service there.

Or I block them and they find a way through with another one and another one and another one in some kind of tennis match: Block number – company forehand return. Block new number – company backhand down the line. Block again – company approaching net – overhead smash: game, set and match.

Or I give up saying 'yes, I had an accident' and without warning I hear a real person awaken, taking over from the artificial intelligence, albeit the real person actually lacks any proper intelligence. 'Yes, I had an accident. It was 27 years ago when I made the error of crashing into (marrying) my wife—' and they inflict further psychological pain by hanging up on me!

Then weeks later I have a real, actual compensation claiming accident to complain about and I don't hear anything from the call chasing cheats.

So, expecting such a call and noticing my roller-coaster driver treat me to a theme park day trip with every corner, traffic light and roundabout abused, I become excited at the thought of being able to talk through an accident in real time. Responding live at the scene as it happens as she pinballs the car off another kerb, ignores the mirrors (which are clearly just in her car to help apply lip gloss) and impressively changes gear again and again just via a determined hand thrust alone – perhaps there isn't a clutch in this car. I return to the call:

"Hi.....yes, I'm about to have an accident. Stay on the line."

"I've got my camera. You ready?"

Partially shocked it's a real person, even a voice I faintly recognise, I hold the phone away from my ear, glance from side to side mouthing 'What?' 'Who?' to my driver as she re-writes *The Highway Code.*

Returning the phone to my ear, "Right   ok who is this?"

"It's Mr Oates of number 69, Private Drive."

Emptying himself with howls of laughter. "It's Lee mate, Lee Oates from uni. I've got my camera. You ready?"

Speaking before thinking: "What the   wow. Mate. It's been years.   Howww   how are you? And what you up to? And how did you get this number?"

"I got it off *Harry Potter. Perfectly normal.*" A shriek of laughter rang out scarring my ears – and forehead. "No, Baz gave it to me really. He's stood to my left wetting himself. I'll put him on. His idea by the way. The call."

Silence. I needed to break it:

"Hello? Baz? You there?"

Baz could not get past the first syllable for crying. I heard him gasping for breath between his raucous roars. Lee shouted in, "We'll see you later. The Nazi has dropped out so I'm taking his place. Baz phoned me last night. Can't wait."

"No, no, I'm ok," Baz interjected. Still laughing between words, "I thought   that   would be   a laugh." Before I had chance to answer, Baz jumped back in, "Eh mate, is Sophie with you?"

"Yeah, she's driving me over. Running bit late."

"Put me on loudspeaker. Go on......"

Knowing you're making a wrong decision but actually going ahead and doing it anyway – is that a common mistake as a man grows older or is it just me?

Bit like last week, in bed, when I knocked on her back door with an enquiring prod and she replied so matter of fact like a newsreader talking to a goldfish in a plant free aquarium, scatter bombing my pride with 'no, not now, flicking through *Bella from last month*. Trish wants the mag back by the weekend.'

Or bit like the last millennium (27 years ago to be exact-ish) when Sophie dive bombed her bumper pack of *PG Tips* into the shopping basket of *Safeway* via her chunkier than mine *DoubleDecker* filled hairy arms and told me she'd missed her monthlies. I did totally the wrong 'right thing' without properly even asking her – it helped that she pushed me over a moment later in the crisp aisle next to the *Monster Munch* and I fell to the floor landing on one knee. Before I could get up, she shouted 'Yes, I will' and it went engagement ring, wedding ring....suffering. In no time we were married and putting pain killers into our trolley.

Maybe I thought she'd improve. Adrian in the *Rocky* movies got considerably better looking with each film. I've heard people say 'never trust Hollywood'. Me Too.

Or bit like last year when I walked into *Kurdish Stans* hairdressers totally sane and just asked for a 'one' all over, deciding to mow my mid-life crisis away without previous consideration. I walked out looking like a golf ball and £14 out of pocket (I'm sure he was just £4.50 when he first set up shop in the UK and mixed in his own dialect with 'What you want boss?' Now he drives a sports car and speaks better English than the English). But he still calls me 'boss'. I only get called 'boss' by two people: hairdressers

and the ones that open my car door and ask 'Inside boss?'
If I just wanted the outside I'd wash it myself but I can't be
bothered to carry an interior hoover to the exterior and
wind out the extension lead so I pay the extra, get the inside
done and get called 'boss'. Back to Baz talking to my boss:

"Soph, my gorgeous little polar bear." He knows
she hates her stumpy white legs that just won't bronze up no
matter how many times she pays for Tanya's half yearly
holidays to the Maldives in return for letting Sophie have
half hour trips to Tanya's '*Glam, Tan and Shimmer Salon*'
in the High Street.

Pulling a vomiting face, "Oh, hi Barry, how are
you?" Her hands off the wheel to demonstrate being sick
into an invisible paper bag. Another kerb rebounded off.

Baz offered a modest proposal: "Eh listen, my
beautiful tiny hippo. I'm due to go on some shit reunion
but I can cancel, pop round to yours. I hear husband is
away. We can drink cheap cider, maybe even treat you to a
snake bite and black. We can play some *Fifa*, yeah, watch a
bit of porn together. Maybe get some kebabs in. You can

re-heat them. Furry Burger. And I'll get you to scream and shout and I'll be all romantic too and buy you a pearl necklace."

"Barry, darling, that, and I am clearly emphasising the word THAT, sounds delightful; just what every woman wants although you forgot to mention the bum slapping, the clothes pegs on my hard nipples, ice cubes inside me and my titties between your tiny brain. Oh, and me writing three letters on your puny little cock."

Baz was confused, "What letters?"

"Let's go for the first letter of my name, the first letter of a typical English drink that's hot but not coffee; could be *Darjeeling* or *Earl Grey* say and the third letter is the letter that used to be on a cone shaped hat placed on your dullard head every day of your shitty school life."

Baz was clearly trying to determine the 2nd and 3rd letters when she finished with: "But actually tonight I'm busy anyway."

"Really? What you doing? Bit early for trick or treating isn't it? Or you at *weight watchers* again?"

Sophie cleared her throat. Never a good sign.

"I'm going anywhere, everywhere with everybody and doing everything – just not with you."

Baz mimicked a laugh. War was declared.

"Ohhhh, Soph, babe, you're blowing me out for a mega girth vibrator on rechargeable everlasting batts. You know I keep telling you that it's a fire extinguisher on my wall you've got your eye on, not a large red dildo."

She loaded. "I would have popped round to see your girlfriend Baz but she said she's got her ex coming round so she'll be busy all night. ALL NIGHT." She fired and hit. Mordant.

I grabbed the phone back.

"I'm at Hoop Corner, be there in 3 mins," I said.

"Fuck sake mate. Hurry up. Everyone should have been here at 8."

"Who else is late?"

"Everyone bar me and Lee so far. I've been here since 7.30 as missus dropped me off early."

Sophie doesn't take prisoners: "Yeah, her ex is coming round for breakfast Baz. Double helping of sausage roll. Extra meaty. And I mean cumin round if you know what I mean!"

The phone hung up. Not sure if it was me or Baz.

"Fuck sake Soph. You know he can't handle the ex thing. He's more emotional than he lets on, especially since the chemo started."

"Well, if your alarm had gone off on time, you'd have already got dropped off and that conversation would never have happened."

"I'm not going to argue right now." I could have. I wouldn't have won. You can't beat the reasoning of the supreme leader. Kim Jong-Soph. Less than one mile left till the drop off when I could claim immunity but I knew she'd soon try to navigate my day ahead with *her* guidance. She always offers this advice, even when I'm just popping down the road to *Harry Webb's newsagents*:

"Tonight, if you're ever not sure what's best, whether to have that kebab, or should you drink that row of shorts, or chat up that vampish tart, or jump that dicey fence, then always remember to ask yourself....."

"Here it comes, out of the shadows...."

"Be quiet and take this advice. Ask yourself, WHAT WOULD CLIFF DO?"

Yes, 'what would Cliff Richard do?' If I'm at logger-heads with myself at any point, I need to pause and ask myself 'what would Cliff Richard do?' She has a love for Cliff that has passed through generations. Her great grand-mother shared the adoration with her daughters who gave it to their daughters who infected Sophie. Sophie once gave 137 cookies to the local church fete, all in the shape and image of Cliff. She had baked 200 but 63 of them were consumed by the chef some way between mixing bowl and church altar. Still, it's the first time Cliff entered over one hundred feasting female mouths.....and incidentally, less than 24 hours later, came out of just as many bottoms.

Sophie started singing '*The Young Ones*'. *Devil Woman*. Three words in, I couldn't take anymore and I spotted a perfect evacuation point. "Drop us here please. I love you." *Saviour's Day*.

"I love you too.   But I'd love you more if you got rid of that alarm clock."

I was out of the car. Nelson Mandela. She pinged the window down as freedom awaited. She is legally entitled to the last word: "Oh, by the way, you've got loads of white toothpaste splattered down the front of your top."

She sped off, hitting another kerb.

4

 University Reunion

 Road Trip

 Stag Party   Celebrating buying a new camera

Incoming Call Number Known.

I wanted to ignore it. She does me. 100 years of

solitude. I'll have to answer it. She won't stop. I don't need
a barrage of pings giving invaluable ammunition to Baz and
the boys as they chainsaw through me – could nail me to a
cross with that ringtone.

Celine Dion '*My Heart Will Go On*'.

We both have the same ringtone just to add more confusion in to our 'dead' lives – the phone explodes with the little French Canadian and neither of us know whose phone it is. Any reluctant gambler passing by *Ladbrokes* will bet on it being hers. She receives thousands of coma inducing calls from 'da girls'. Her latest radicicolous device with a re-mortgage of a phone contract is generally glued to her whilst I often lose my brick; or Celine's opening boom eradicates the last 2% of battery I have left on it. Oh, and as if I could should would forget, we also have this identical ringtone as it was our wedding song. A slow torturous uncoordinated affair that wouldn't be humane viewing in Guantanamo Bay. Sex on the dancefloor it certainly wasn't. I was the Titanic and she was the iceberg. With eternal thanks to a scratchy bit of Dion vinyl, the DJ slapped on the Macarena two minutes in.

"Hi Sophie."

Silence. Relieved no concerning accidents have occurred and the air bag hasn't gone off.

Then it does:

"You know you've only got one shirt."

"No, I've got a spare Sophie. I put the chequered one in."

"No, I took that out. I don't like that on you."

"uhhh,   it doesn't matter you don't like the bloody thing as you're not coming on the trip. You won't se---."

"No, I still like you to look your best   so did you not put another one in?"

"   Why would I replace a shirt that I didn't know had been taken out in the first place? Jeeez. I don't believe it."

"No need to get like all angry." She should have said 'all shirty'. "You should have replaced it whether you knew or not."

I paused to decipher her *Da Vinci Code* reasoning. "No probs. I'll just borrow one."

"Ok, well, it won't be the plain mauve one I like."

"It can be if you want to pop into the house, jump into the wardrobe avoiding the lion and the witch and bring it over."

. "Ha, ha, very funny. No, I don't but have a nice time anyway," and she went. Vanished. Narnia? No. Probably just off to eat Turkish Delight or more likely, start and finish a box of '*Celebrations*'.

Calmness punched me and forgot where I was.

"Was that the missus ringing you already?" Baz beckoned me over from the other side of the street. Behind him, Lee was already filming but with one hand up encouraging me to wave. I did.

Baz, a mix of excitement and anxiety, proceeded to ask question after question with no passes and no correct answers:

"This is going to be a laugh today isn't it? Where the hell is everyone? Bell must beonhisway do you reckon?

Chinny and Khan won't drop out willthey? Where the fuck the minibus? You   alright   then? God, whatTIMEisit? You know Steve the Nazi ain't coming don't you?"

"Mate, mate, relax. All will be fine." Baz nodded but continued to glance between his watch and the empty roads, no doubt looking for signs of good times ahead.

I'd forgotten Lee was there. He soon zoomed in and I greeted him. "Put that camera down you twat. Lee, it's been years." We shook hands which evolved into a hug which devolved into a couple of back slaps before we took synchronised reverse steps, both shaking our heads muttering '27 years, eh, wow, 27 years'.

Something was needed to distract us from the embarrassment of two middle aged blokes reluctantly cuddling (whilst one of them held a camera aloft panning towards Baz who was now pacing up and down the road, stepping on and off the pavement, almost wishing the others to appear). Something did happen. Celine came back onstage.

"Fuck me mate. Answer that before it kills a couple of cats," Baz said glancing at his own phone (it said the same time as his watch).

I'm a great *Great Gatsby* fan, I'd have a Great Gatsby purple scarf if I could and chant 'come on you Gatsby' from the terraces every Saturday afternoon before going home and watching Gatsby Lineker present 'Chapter of the Day'. It would just be minimal highlights I know. I'd just get the odd paragraph here or there – the programme would always open with Dickens City or Shakespeare United and I'd have to wait till the end for snippets of Fitzgerald Hotspur.

I scrolled across to receive her call. As I heard her first word, a bit of the GG came to mind:

In my younger and less vulnerable years, my father gave me some advice. He said if your wife ever rings up and reminds you that you've got toothpaste on your shirt, don't repeat her words out loud because the others with you will take it down and use it in evidence against you. His wise words were really: 'criticism of an error is fair so don't make the single error a pair.'

"Hi Sophie. What's up?"

"Nothing. Have you borrowed a shirt yet?"

"No, not y—"

"I'm ringing to remind you in case you forgot about the toothpaste on your top."

"Yeah, course. I know I've got toothpaste on my top."

Toothpaste on my top was my first error. Repetition of her words was the pair. The top and the toothpaste were now on Baz's banter radar. Cut the call. "You're cracking up.   I can't hear you." End call.

"Eh, eh, let's look at your top. Whooooaaaa. Fuck sake. Hilarious. Eh, Lee, film this," Baz declared poking my top and with increased volume even though Lee was stood right next to him.

Shrugging my shoulders, "just toothpaste mate. Not exactly *comedy central* or the *Dave* channel."

"Bollox mate." Looking at camera, "Look, he's got cum all over his top."

Baz needed to distract himself from the pending mental breakdown with none of the others yet to arrive – he started to wave down cars, shout at artic lorries and even beckon over a young pram pushing mother who was on her phone (in the pram there was a large ipad and it was holding a small baby).

"He's got cum on his top.

Shirt of Spunk.

Jizzzz Jumperrrr.

Splooey Mayo Man."

We were saved from any more of Baz's 'toothpaste' shout-outs regarding the human stain as we all stopped in our tracks and gazed in astonishment. Frozen in time. Only Lee's camera kept rolling. The three of us were on 'pause'.

Out of the exhaust fumes rolled 2 suitcases with a human figure between them. A male body wrapped in a union jack morphsuit. Imagine a red, white and blue rotting cucumber swamped in clingfilm. Hardly patriotic is it?

5

☑ University Reunion

☑ Road Trip

☒ Stag Party ☑ Celebrating buying new camera

☑ 50th birthday

Now there were four of us. One of us (Lee)

wasn't even originally invited (till last night). Chinny had just

arrived in a morphsuit. Most meretricious. We knew it was

Chinny as he had a bit of a Jimmy Hill. Chinny, aka Ed

Nooteboom was once called 'Jawbones Nonary'. This was

due to the contours of his face and because he played

number nine for the university football team but Chinny

rolled off all our *Desperate Dan* tongues better than

Jawbones Nonary). That Chinny muzzle protruding from his all in one outfit was easily recognisable. He needed a trowel to shave that beauty of a chin. Fortunately, nothing else seemed to be sticking out near his equator.

Now it was well past *breakfast* and we were far from *champions* but I suppose one could say that *this is now a tale of four lonesome (far from skinny) fairly old mutli-coloured men on a planet whose day trip was dying fast.*

We all wanted to ask. None of us did at first. We initiated contact as soon as Chinny unzipped his morph head piece, a cloth helmet armouring his head. It would have been difficult talking to what appeared like a walking mannequin – we all knew Bell had once been arrested in *Debenhams* mid 90's for trying to mount a mannequin at 5 to 5 on a Friday afternoon – not exactly *crackerjack*!

Baz interacted with our very own extra-terrestrial: "Why you wearing that?"

"Fancy dress innit," Chinny replied joyfully.

"Ah, um   NO. Basically no mate. But wear what you want."

"You bloody Chaucerian queynte. You told me it was fancy dress," Chinny replied less joyfully.

"Yeah it was originally. I changed it. You not get the message?"

"Clearly not.   Oh, so what," he said blowing out air. "I'll keep it on. I'm 50 soon so what the 'ell."

"Yeah, good man. You can get changed into normal clothes mid-way up there anyway. You got other clothes yeah?"

"I have but just two other fancy dress outfits."

"What? You got two suitcases either side of you." Pointing at two shiny large cases.

One case had a huge 'T' in marker pen written on it. The other had a red 'L' designed to look like a 'Learner' badge.

"Yeah, Thelma," tapping the slightly larger one, "is packed full of beer plus one *baby sham*. Louise has just got the vodka and my two other outfits."

"Yo man. You absolute star. Let's crack 'em open," Baz erupted whilst fondling Thelma, quickly launching out a beer to each of us with an underhand primary school rounders style throw.

"Don't you want to know what my other outfits are?" Chinny said opening his beer.

"Oh yeah, what you got? Lee asked.

"Nothing major. Nothing John Major either." He slapped his foot down. No one laughed. "I've got this morphsuit, a basic Jesus one and the old Chinny special."

"Not the fireman suit?"

"Yep, 100% guaranteed to unreel the hose and spray a hot bird. Or rather attract the attention of someone totally liquidated who likes firemen suits. Though I have to call it the firefighter suit nowadays to be PC and all that.

Ha, just thought a PC outfit would be PC. Get it? Police Constable PC." Only one person laughed this time. Chinny himself. "Anyway, forget that shit." Chinny clashed his beer against Lee's. "Lee, I didn't even know you were coming. Bloody awesome to see you. Last I heard you'd married a Malaysian woman."

Lee started to reply, "Ye---" when Chinny immediately spun 180 degrees,

"......and you......" He pointed at me and started to almost mimic the twist n' shout jive dance, swinging his hips and alternating his arms at me, "great to see you again too – nice load of cum on your top." No chance to reply as Chinny spun 360 degrees asking, "Where's Khan, Nazi boy Steve and the Bell End? Anyone got the QP and KM trophies?

"No idea who has the QP and KM awards. Probably lost in someone's attic. No Steve Stevenson. He dropped out. Khan? He must be here soon. As for Bell? Not sure where that big burrowing mammal is? He's probably got his long ears, his tubular snout and his extensive tongue feeding inside some termites pants."

Just as Baz said that, a black London taxi pulled up.

Definitely not Bell.

Out stepped a sanguine Imran-Ahab Anand who was better known as Khan at uni. Terse and polished, escalating towards nabob status and in his best bib and tucker. 'Khan' was the only Asian bloke at our uni back in the 90's and we gave him the nickname of the only Asian bloke we knew with the name Imran: Imran Khan. Next to him was what looked like a gorgeous model, a nubile girl barely perhaps 21 years of age who looked like something out of Bollywood. She'd win you the QP trophy forever.

So stunning, so beautiful.   Too young.

Maybe it's best Bell doesn't turn up.

6

 University Reunion

 Road Trip

 Stag Party　　 Celebrating buying new camera

 50th birthday (~~fancy dress party~~)

 New Job

The girl was diffident, standing next to the taxi,

continually looking down on to the pavement. Khan paid the taxi fare. Always happy to flash the cash. His accountant is a *fleismaster* butchering his investments to shinplasters and rendering his wallet financially incapacitated. Khan always bounces back. We all walked over. The girl getting younger and less plausible as every heart palpitation passed. We queued up to greet him.

Khan has never been short of a few quid. He buys bottled water, brand new cars, tinned tuna masquerading as cash diluting caviar and takeaways each evening – he's the personification of opulent. He likes the finer things in life, one of which I'd agree with. He's always had an allegiance to the *National Trust.* Chinny doesn't even know what the NT is. National Front is more his annual subscription club. Lee on the other hand, with all his diagnoses, ailments and mystery illnesses is National Health Service. Lee's been so much, he reviews it on *Trip Advisor.*

"Khan, you rich bastard. You get a taxi all the way from Central London?"

"Baz, good to see you man."

The queue proceeded to greet the Great Khan.

"Khan, been a few years but you look the same."

"Chinny. Same big chin I see. What's with the morph suit? Actually, don't tell me."

"Khan, always good to see you mate," I said feeling genuinely pleased I was reacquainting myself with all these old mates.

"Eh, still with Sophie no doubt? Still trying to play cricket and missing middle wicket no doubt no doubt?"

"Yep," as if I needed to answer.

"Got a bit of seaman on your top," Khan said in such a way that it almost felt dignified.

"Khan, I'm here coz Steve dropped out. I'm filming it for posterity. I could be in Naseby re-enacting the English Civil War, dressed as a Cavalier but I couldn't m—"

"You're a Royalist eh? That must make Bell a roundhead with his fat face, and yeah, I heard about the Nazi. This was supposed to be his stag party and he couldn't even make it himself. Good to see you still have a camera in your hand. Just no posting me on social media. Got a new job. Not good for the company image seeing me with my head down a toilet Lee."

"Your head down a toilet?" Baz shouted. "More like your face in some fanny you old Sultan of the City. The Gravy Sikh as we called you. Always going down for the gravy."

"Whoaaa, whoaa, whoa." Imran started nodding across to the young girl who was still looking like she was waiting for a bus, moving her feet about to just look like she wasn't doing nothing. "This is my daughter."

We all turned. Open mouthed. The daughter raised a timid smile.

"Don't embarrass her. She's embarrassed enough by me already. And she goes red quick. Not easy for someone with an Indian dad and a white mum."

"Ha, ha," Baz quickly added wanting to get to the point the rest of us had mused. "So, what's she doing here?"

"Oh right, well, ummm, I forgot to tell her mum I was away and as you know we're not together anymore – I blame the grandparents. Mixed marriage and all that."

"Blame the grandparents? Blame the short skirted high heeled treacle tart of a secretary or blame the pin striped shiny shoed Khan who couldn't resist rolling her pastry I'd say, "said Baz, adding, "just what I read on social media," winking, "no offence like. I call it *Restorative* – Khan gets most of his secretary and Khan's wife gets most of the house, and the dogs, and the car and the timeshare in Ibiza. Just what I read in the court documents," winking twice, "no offence like. *They say the penis mightier than the words.*"

Sensing a spike in the tension, I returned to the original question. "So, how come your daughter is here now? Is she staying with friends or family locally? You are coming aren't you Khan?"

"Oh yeah. I'm definitely not missing this one," he said as Baz patted him on the back and passed him a beer.

"Thing is, my daughter has to tag along." Baz pulled the beer back.

"What? Eh? Am I missing something?" He turned to Khan's daughter. "Sorry love, not being rude and all that but this is a jolly boys outing. Four walls and all that. What's going on Khan?"

"She's only 17. 18 tomorrow. Wow, 18 years ago she came out by caesarean covered in blood and not breathing. Then she saw me, cried and was alive. Best present I've ever had."

"Yeah, carry on," Baz said.

"She's only with me every other weekend. I can't leave her home alone at mine, since, well, ummmm, she, ah, well, she just can't be left alone.   So, she's on the bus. Everyone ok?"

Everyone paused. Probably waiting for Baz. Baz isn't really respected as a decision maker. He struggles deciding whether to drink from a glass or a bottle – and that's with milk, not beer.

But he has organised this, so I suppose we all thought he'll 'yes' it or 'no' it. Should she stay or should she go? Baz temporised no longer:

"Yeah, no problem. We'll get a diet cola for her when we stop eh   or does she drink like her dad?" Everyone chuckled. Even Khan's daughter.

Baz tried to make Khan's daughter feel at home. "So, welcome aboard the bus, when it finally gets here. Watch out for Bell if he finally gets here."

"What's your name?" Lee asked. "Did your dad give you a proper Sikh name like   ah   like   um...."

Clearly fumbling over his dictionary of Indian female names, I helped him out. "Prisha or Salena maybe?"

"Knowing Khan, he probably called you something stupid," Baz laughed. "He loved his 90's music so something like Kylie or Shania. Cher maybe. Not Bjork no? What you called? Nothing stupid we hope!"

"Alexa," she said.

There was a moment when mouths were moving but words weren't coming out. Then.

"Alexa?" Chinny asked. "Where's this sodding bus and shuffle songs by Iron Maiden." Everyone laughed. Even Alexa. Chinny started singing '*Bring Your Daughter to the Slaughter.*"

Khan stopped laughing.

7

 University Reunion

 Road Trip

 Stag Party    Celebrating buying new camera

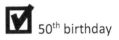 50th birthday

 New Job

 18th Birthday

Incoming Automobile. Passenger Known.

A car with almost as many dents as my marriage hurtled towards the group and braked. The sudden attention seeking stop was amplified by a detonation of horn beeping. The vehicle had so many modifications – any car insurance quote would have been a minefield of questions. I had two questions: Why are there a pair of fluffy blue whales hanging in the front window next to dice and is that really a dildo glued to the front bonnet??

The passenger leaned over and consumed the driver. We couldn't tell who was who. One face was plunging another – a pair of suction cup muzzle chops. Their passionate and extended goodbye resembled two octopuses wrestling with each other. Eventually they stopped. They started again. More the *Blind Assassin* and a *Comedy of Errors* than *Lady Chatterley's Lover* – the only liaisons dangereuses about this 'au revoir' was the hand-brake was off and the car started rolling. Bell escaped and

'*Lolita*' or whoever she was, hit the brakes, and then hit the accelerator leaving yet more skid marks.

"Oi, Oi, Saveloy." He leaves no duvet uncovered and no female lonely. This was Bell. The man without qualities. Body by *The Addams Family*. Brain by *Fisher-Price*. Nickname Bell End. Christened (but clearly rejected by religion) Bell Rice. His parents had no comprehension of how to give your firstborn son a name. His younger brothers are called Jeremy, Mark and Tom. Normal. His one and only sister has the 'normal' name of Beatrice. Sounds normal. Then you realise she's called Beatrice Rice. We don't think they abused or beat Beatrice Rice. Even his first dog was called Samson – then they called the next one Jalfrezi.

Put Bell in a scrum and he'll die for the team. Women find him attractive. A mix of a man's man and a giant sex toy for desperate women; all rolled in to one big bald wall. No one can live with him though he is responsible – if anything goes wrong, Bell is often the one responsible. Definitely juvenal and juvenile. He longs for just three things: alcohol, women and sleep; often in that order. He'll eat bread but he's never been to a circus. He's a lioness tamer (and a clown).

He sums up the word 'belly-god' as no one finds greater pleasure in gratifying their appetite.

Bell was the first grain of the Rice family to get to university. No one really knows how he got in. A levels? He's got two D's and an unclassified. Yes, Bell's a DUD. O levels? If there was such a thing as a Grade G, then he'd have got CABBAGE. Bell would get a 'fail' for common sense – he once told me the 100 Years war was 116 years. No idea how he made university. We think he got some kind of secret sports scholarship for rugby. We'll never know.

Chinny started a rumbustious chant:

"He's fat,

He's round,

His balls bounce on the ground.

Belly Rice, Belly Rice."

Three verses, the latter two of which Bell himself joined in. Baz stood back waiting.

"Sorry I'm late but that girl is insatiable." Bell had an amphitheatre of attention, a horseshoe of followers waiting on his every word. Even Khan seemed interested to hear what was coming next. Only Baz remained at a distance, away from Bell's soapbox.

It was reminiscent of the *Summer Loving* grandstand scene out of '*Grease*'. Chinny even said 'Tell Me More'. I'm sure Bell would have sung 'she was good, you know what I mean, she was cute and only 18 stone' if he'd have thought of it.

"She just kept coming back for more   or rather going down for more, eh, eh. I nicknamed her '*Dyson*'. She sucks like a vacuum cleaner. She went down on me so many times, she asked for a loyalty card. I know I'm fat but it was like parting the red sea, jumping in and riding the waves with her thighs." Bell was receiving a few chuckles but most were shaking their heads slowly whilst breaking a smile.

"I should have called her Robin as she was red breasted by the end of our sess."

Alexa was stood open mouthed in a similar fashion to that which Darwin must have been when he came across a strain of a new breed.

Alexa had no intention of cataloguing the origin of this new species.

"It was good. I know it was because the sex sounded like someone running in flip flops." Bell ejaculated his words before continuing. "I'll name that bedtime story as The Snail Trail and the Whale." Bell erupted in laughter and all except Baz cracked up in the aftershocks. A red hell was bearing down on Baz. Angry and angrier.

I glanced back at Bell in full flow re-telling more of his adventures of a plumber's mate. He was wearing a slightly torn and vomit stained T-shirt which read 'sex, weights and a protein shake'. For a man that looks like he's never frequented a gym, a more suitable T-shirt slogan may have been 'wanking, cake and a belly ache'. But this was a man who looked and smelt like a Cess Pitt but got more female attention than Brad Pitt. Bell gets four or five Valentines cards every year without fail. He'd get a lot more but most of his acquaintances can't read or write.

I returned to his laddish monologue.

"I wouldn't have been late but she insisted on going round the back way."

"There is no back way from your house to here Bell. It's just one straight road."

"I'm not talking roads Chinny. But if I was, she'd be a bloody dual carriageway. She bored me something silly about cosmetic surgery as she's saving up for lip fillers. I offered her a mouth filler. Free of charge."

"Can't believe she gave you the key to her backdoor Bell?"

"I didn't unlock her though. I couldn't even take the bra off. I knew I shouldn't have worn it."

"Mate, sounds like you've been well fed," Khan noted hoping to put an end to Bellend's chat.

"I am a bit partial to snacking," Bell said, smiling and patting his stomach, hiding a small double decker bus, "but that girl was *Kit-Kat.*"

"Uh? *Kit-Kat?*" Khan asked intrigued.

"Four fingers mate." There was a moment of stillness. Only Bell could abolish his own period of calm. "It was like Kafka's *Metamorphosis.* Kafka never finished his own book. I've finished every beetle bonnet I've started........

I awake and find myself transformed in her bed next to a monstrous gigantic insect.

I had to get out. It was bon voyage instead of bondage. I'm only here for a rest. I was like a jack-knifed lorry at the mercy of her desires. Can't blame her really. She called me Moses at the end."

"Why Moses?" Khan asked.

"She had a burning bush mate. No doubt she's already missing me. Probably now driving home, straddling seats and sitting on the gear stick. Insatiable." There was no stopping him. His crowd was listening less, starting to snooze but he had to continue. Ken Dodd. And his diddy man. And his tickle stick. "I had to get out. Otherwise it would have been naked lust and naked lunch all day. She won't give me syphilis. I got that from Girolamo FracastWhateverHisName-Is. Let's just hope she isn't Cheggers Plays Pop."

"Cheggers Plays Pop?" asked Lee.

"Cheggers! Preggers like!" Bell replied introducing Lee to the first chapter of his Bell Jar-gon. "The last one is pregs. I'm going to be a dad again in five and a half months. I can't have this one having a *baby Bell* as well, especially as I was all cheesy this morning." He almost collapsed laughing; stopping himself from keeling over by putting his hands on his wide knees.

"And if she does have your baby, then you'll be related to Baz," Chinny said. I then realised that this driver

'*Lolita*' was actually Baz's sister Delores. This was enough to break Baz's self-imposed vow of silence:

"You're a great bloke mate but no way I want you as my brother in law," Baz said diplomatically.

"Eh Baz, your sister's lovely really. Sorry about all the roly poly jibes but you know I only say 'em coz I like her and coz I'm not exactly slim shady myself and coz I'm not thinking straight. I'm like hungover."

"You had a load of drinks last night did you Bell?" Chinny asked.

"A couple of beers, then shared a red but I mean hungover from all that riding. She's like a bloody hippo. Sausage jockey. She made me wear her knickers when I was leaving so I could smell her all day."

"Fucks sake that's sick," Khan said looking away as Bell pulled the one side of his jeans down a bit to reveal pink lace.

"Trouble is, they're baggy on me."

That was the moment that Baz's inner fury vanished.

"You bastard Bell. Even I think that's funny," Baz wiped his brow. "At least if you're with my sister, you're not dipping it in your own sister." Baz jabbed Bell in the arm joking. "That other girl you dated was YOUR sister Bell."

"Sheena? She wasn't MY sister. My dad and her mum got together."

"Stepsister then. Same thing. Investment in incest I'd say."

"Sheena Bohica wasn't even a stepsister Baz. My dad was with her mum for a couple of weeks, a month tops. BUT what I do remember is one evening I was with Sheena watching a romantic movie---"

"Like *Robocop*?" Chinny interjected.

".....when Delores, your sis Baz, knocked on the door. Awkward at first but then I gave in   and the rest is *Sistory* as they say. Sister sandwich with extra salad cream."

"Pity that sister on the bottom with you and the other one on top of that sister sandwich," I said.

"Flat bread more like," Chinny added.

I've heard Bell share his sister-story before. He refers to them all as the three musketeers. The three little pigs is two thirds accurate. When it comes to numbers, accuracy is not always essential. There are, according to some, 256 shades of grey; and don't ask Bell how many children he has.

"How many kids you got Bell?" Khan asked.

"A few. I always wanted a football team of my own. I even wanted to have a child with dual nationality."

"Like being British and Irish? Two passports?"

"Yeah, but Welsh and English would have done me. I took my first girlfriend Rusty away to a place called Tref-y-Clawdd, half the town in England, the other half in

Wales. We did it on a footbridge near a river right on the border in the depths of the night. My one foot was in Wales and the other foot in England." Bell started acting out the horror, lumping his feet apart and starting to thrust his body backwards and forwards.

"Stop that," Khan said. "It's not where the baby is conceived anyway. It's where it's born that counts for nationality. Where is this Tref-y-Clawdd anyway?"

"Right on the border like I said. Tref-y-Clawdd. Translates to 'town on the dyke'. Turned out it was 'Bell on the dyke' as it happens as when we got home, Rusty went off with a butch security guard called Cheryl."

"What?" Khan laughed. "One weekend away with you and she turned lesbian. Brilliant." After all, oranges are not the only fruit – not for Bell, our very own gingerbread man.

Baz was feeling like more action, less words: "Right, enough of this. We're all here. Let's get going."

There was a new excitement within the group. I should have called the register:

King, Oates, Rice, Anand, Nooteboom.

Chinny collected T & L, handing out a new set of beers. Khan loosened his tie and gave Lee a couple of pats on the shoulder. Bell and Baz embraced. I realised things were looking good. Then Alexa fucked it all up:

"Excuse me dad,   and Baz I guess   sorry to umm   interrupt," she said with reluctance, looking around the vehicle free car park, "just wondered,   where's the bus?"

"Ah Bollox," Baz said looking up at the cloud looming sky. He kicked out at fresh air and walked several metres into a beer-less, person-less, minibus-less space to make a call.

"Right, better crack open that vodka," Chinny said holding both hands up in front of him. Pouring large help-ings into paper cups, we saw Baz in the distance remonstrat-ing with someone the other end of his mobile phone. We were too far away to hear any words but it was looking like we'd be completing the vodka before Baz '*russianed*' back over.

"So," Chinny asked, "how did you meet that Malaysian wife Lee?"

Lee took a swig. "I bought her." We all took a swig. Chinny semi-filled all the paper cups and gave Lee a bit extra.

"Yeah," Lee continued, "I went over there on an organised trip. Me and about 20 or so others but they were all single, rich, old men all in their 50's, 60's, 70's even."

"Man, you must have been like a youthful David Beckham being the young stallion compared with all those old geezers."

"Not exactl---"

"I bet they loved you. Were you batting them away?"

"Opposite mate. The Malaysian women thought I was one of the old boys' grand kids just there for the holiday. Then they realised and I was last in line because they all thought I was just a poor young chap   which I was which I still half am. But then this lady organising it from their side took a shine to me and it all happened. 20 years on and we're still happy and still in love."

"Nice one mate. Fair play to you."

"Funny thing is I went out there to buy a beautiful young Malaysian wife, someone that would have won me the QP lifetime achievement award and I ended up with one for free and she was almost twice my age."

Lee got out a photograph.

"She's beautiful mate, " Chinny said.

"Yeah stunning," I added.

"Good looker that mate," Bell said, "but I can see she's a lot older yeah."

Lee popped the photo back in his wallet.

"And with her being foreign, she doesn't pick up on my *Aspergers syndrome* autism stuff so she's the only person in the world I know who thinks I'm normal."

Baz stomped back over swearing.

"I've fucked up sorry guys."

"What's up Baz? Is the bus not booked?" I asked.

"Oh no, it's booked all right."

Bell nodded approvingly.

"It's booked. It's coming. Just it's coming tomorrow."

Bell spat out his vodka but caught most of it in his hands, licking his fingers before suggesting, "Right all down the Duck and Duke, then back same time tomorrow."

Everyone was considering it before I reminded them, "We're going to Coventry for that Saturday night over 35's nightclub remember? Tomorrow is Sunday. It will be closed."

"I'll sort it," Baz said.

"What, get 'em to open the club up tomorrow?" asked Bell.

"Chinny, look up some bus company numbers," Baz said bouncing.

Khan wandered off. Bell started drinking straight from the vodka bottle.

"Why are we going to Coventry anyway? I thought most people get sent there when they did something wrong."

"The record for the most people in a single pair of underpants ever is 314 and was set in Coventry," our very own Captain Underpants (Lee) said before adding, "in case anyone is interested."

I was thinking 'I bet they were one of Bell ex's knickers (aka parachutes) for the record attempt when the very man lamented:

"I should be in the *Guinness Book of Records* for two reasons but I'm not."

No one bothered to reply so he replied to himself:

"Why's that Bell? I'll tell you why. Very interesting actually and thanks for asking. Reason one is when I was born I was the youngest person in the world." No one acknowledged him. "Reason two is I once owned the record for the fastest individual hand jive to the *Grease* music." Anyone that can do a complicated pattern of hand moves incorporating fist pounding, hand clapping, crossing the wrists and hitch hike moves resembling an elaborate version of pat-a-cake needed to show us before we edged towards the hand job jokes. Before any of us could give an automatic systematic hydromatic lightning strike of recognition, Khan came back into sight. Rushing up the road, panting out of breath.

"Need to get down the gym mate," Bell said.

"Ha. Only time you've ever done runs is a Monday morning after eating the Sunday dinners splashed up by your mum when you've had diarrhoea mate."

"I'm in shape. I do 25 push-ups a day Khan," Bell said pointing at his right arm.

"Not intentionally. You just fall over a lot. And yes, you're in 'shape' – round is a shape."

"Ah ok," Bell acknowledged. "I don't gym it for one reason. Listen. A tortoise doesn't run and does nothing and lives for 450 years. Learn from nature I say."

Baz and Chinny came back. "Everything's booked up. Nothing. Not one bus."

"Doesn't matter," Khan said, "I've just stopped a bloke with a big white van. He'll take us to Coventry."

"You bloody beauty," Baz gasped. "Thank God."

"Don't thank God. Don't even thank Godiva. Thank Khan!" Khan said proudly god-gifu like.

8

☑ University Reunion

☑ Road Trip

☒ Stag Party   ☑ Celebrating buying new camera

☑ 50th birthday

☑ New Job

☑ Just here for the beer

☑ 18th birthday

W e rounded the corner. Foaming 40% volume

from the mouth. A pack of re-excited wolves; there was a newly ignited passion oozing from us (plus a clear distilled alcoholic beverage infiltrating our bodies with permission). Six middle aged men; one stained in vomit, another bludgeoned with toothpaste; and an out of place teenage daughter plus two roller skating suitcases.

In front of us, squeezing itself half upon the pavement, camouflaging double yellow lines was an un-marked white van, covered in dust and begging to be blazoned with 'clean me'.

"Not exactly *Actaen Luxury Travel* minibus hire with on board mini bar and LED tv's," Baz groaned.

A dark-haired giant of a man with a pot holed face was adjacent to the van. He appeared to be feverously argu-ing with the person on the other end of his phone when suddenly, another phone rang. He expelled this new phone from his torn back pocket and lifted this to his ear. Slightly withdrawing the other original phone, he shouted, 'Fuck off', aggressively closing the call and returning the phone to his pocket. He resumed the original call, speaking in what appeared to be an Eastern European accent. 'Fuck off' is clearly asperento-ish, a universal language. Mid-way through his verbal scuffle, he acknowledged us all, but gave more recognition to the bottles of vodka Chinny held, almost greeting them as friends. He smiled. The inside of his mouth could have bitten through barbed wire. His bucket sized hands signalled 'two in front, rest in back'. That's what we assumed. Perhaps he was indicating 'two of you will live, the rest in the back of the death van'. We were grateful for the lift, shit scared of our tour guide. We were doing whatever he signalled.

Bell shouted 'shotgun' and attempted to open the passenger side. The driver understood the word 'gun' as he mimed a rifle, accurate in his shoulder tight grip, squeezing the trigger and pointing at Bell with a quick twitch of the head to go in the back. Maybe he saw Bell (being six foot two, heavy and equally brutish) as a threat should (when) he decides to kill us all. Or maybe he knew of Bell's reputation as an odour exiting bottom belcher. Either way, Khan and his daughter were pointed towards the seats upfront. The rest of us lined up as cattle by the rear doors.

My phone buzzed. I had it on silent vibrate. My heart will go on but my ears are preserved. Awaiting certain and quick immediate mortality at the hands of our *Dastardly* Eastern European driver seemed favourable compared to the slow painful suffering I felt at the claws of my *Muttley* Western European wife.

"What time you back tomorrow?" she said without pauses.

"I've no idea," I replied realising the journey back into deep space tomorrow could be as challenging as the lift off yet to occur.

TEN NINE EIGHT

"Well, you've got the fish to do."

SEVEN

This weekly Sunday morning occupation almost en-couraged me to start going to church. Each sabbath day, we would 'bond as a couple' (as she describes it) by cleaning out the fish tank. In one week, the six little fin wagging (or are there five now after one 'floated' this week?) make the inside of their tank as dirty as the outside of a mud moving Somme suffering *Panzer*. Only Bell swimming in and out of the plastic rocks himself would shit more. So, she rolls her sleeves up and wipes the glass with a sponge before I have the dishonour of sucking up a bucket full of fish faeces. Rarely do I swallow the liquid from this tank. Rarely did she swallow the liquid from my tank's gun.

Bonding.

"Yeah, I'll be home tomorrow," I said scribing S.O.S. on the grime covered rear of the van.

SIX FIVE

"Ok great. Gotta go. Just had a blast of notifications come in from my Mission Upgrade Gym Swimmers *whatsapp* group."

FOUR

She gets incredibly excited over any notification. I named her 'fitness with the girls' *whatsapp* group the 'Mission Upgrade Gym Swimmers' for her and she still doesn't realise I acronym'd them 'MUGS'. Well, the first few times they went on their special offer free membership pay £62 a month deal, they used the gym, did a spin class, went for a swim (albeit breast stroke head above water synchronised rubbish talk) and used the 'healthy' café after – probably 3 or 4 times per week. Now they go once every other week, quick walk on the running machine, jacuzzi, sauna and 12 bicep curls sipping a latte. Divide £62 by 2. Simple math. £31 a visit. And she almost paid extra for a personal trainer.

"In," said the driver.

THREE

The doors opened jarringly – the noise of chalk on a 1970's blackboard came to mind. It was pitch black inside, rudimentary comfort but we could make out a *Jenga* of boxes ahead.

"You a courier?" asked Baz nervously as he stepped up to the door. There's no way he'll understand the word 'courier' I thought. If Baz had asked him, 'do you sell body parts for fun?' he may have understood.

One thing's for sure this bloke doesn't work in an office. The driver grabbed Baz by the leg and Baz was frozen awaiting his fate.

"I not courier. I work in an office in Lithuania."

"Lithuania? There's 6.7 murders per 100,000 people," Lee whispered in my ear. There's six of us. Alexa can be the point seven. We're all fucked.

"But at weekends I earn extra money for my wife and babies by delivering yes."

The driver, the killer, Mr Stalin Mussolini of Baghdad with his razor-sharp molars and arms made in less than £62 a month gyms of Lithuania is really *Eleanor Oliphant.*

When people ask what I do, Baz and dental hygienists, I tell them I work in an office.

I got in the bus thanking our family man - two jobs - saviour for his kindness. We were going to Coventry. I held on to the back of Chinny's morphsuit; making extra sure I was holding the suit and nothing within it. We were a chain gang of middle-aged men finding our way through darkness, past boxes of genuine goods and we sat down finally aware that our day was finally singing.

TWO

"Right, who wants a beer?" Chinny said.

"Yeaaaassss pleeeeeese." It was none of us.

"Yeaaaassss pleeeeeese," said a voice again from the other side of the van. "We all av beer if you offar."

I don't know who jumped first but because we were all tight, packed and wired together, hands on our knees, one electrified jump sent us all into high voltage. Baz triggered his phone torch and directed it towards the far side of the van. There sat in a squeezed panoramic row of startled Peking ducks were six oriental men all covered in blankets.

"We appy to av beer wif you."

ONE

The engine started.

LIFT OFF.

We were on our rocket van to Coventry.

9

☑ University Reunion

☑ Road Trip

☒ Stag Party ☑ Celebrating buying new camera

☑ 50th birthday

☑ New Job

☑ Just here for the beer

☑ 18th birthday

☑ Welcome to the UK ceremony x6

☑ Delivering goods to make money for his family

Thirty minutes in. Beer bottles clinked. Vodka shared in the darkness. The back of the van was banging. Feng-shui.

International relations were progressing. The *pride* of two nations *and* no *prejudice.*

It is a truth universally acknowledged that a group of men in possession of empty stomachs must be in want of some fast food.

We felt the van slow, swerve a little, brake and come to a jolting standstill. Not one drop of vodka was spilled. We heard voices. Not Lithuanian. Not Khan's. Not Alexa's voice. Their driver and passenger doors opened. Footsteps. The back doors of the van sprung back. Light. Piercing. Jeez, not again, I thought. Noses moving in one direction. Lips in another. Groundhog Day. Just this time Sophie wasn't reading aloud.

"Everyone out." The driver growled. "22 mins then back here." He's one of these people that probably shouts bedtime stories to his little kids. He screeches whispers. I was looking forward to hearing him bellow for a cappuccino.

An older couple, their car stuttering to move, gawped; startled as a mixed bag of 11 men leapt from the back of the van and splintered off towards the services. I waved at the couple who had aged further in seconds. Neither waved back. She was clambering for something in her handbag. He'd only taken his hands off his steering wheel (his fingers wrapped around it firm) to internally lock the doors.

The services were bustling with hungry travellers – walking, peeing, talking, eating, queuing and drinking – sometimes all at the same time. The sounds of credit cards cashing, burgers flipping, cisterns flushing, plastic recycling and an *AA* man asking if we'd be interested in breakdown cover. That van needs more roadside assistance yes, but I went to drain my own radiator fluid.

I returned from the toilets. Two of our Chinese cousins were rummaging in *WH Smiths*, heads devoured within a Jeremy Clarkson book. A group of bus trip pensioners were pointing at Chinny in his morph suit. They were giggling, amazed at his stupidity before they got back on their coach for their turkey and tinsel weekend in June. Bell was seventh in line for fast food. Khan and his daughter had skipped the queues and were walking back with an array of healthy-looking tofu trays. A greying man in his 60's tapping buttons in the fruit machine area was firing pound coin after pound coin into the slot. Revolving cherries. It was eating his money. His forehead leaned against the screen and he treated the machine to an assertive forearm slap. It wasn't his lucky day. Then a woman, looking much younger, perhaps in her early 30's, swept in, gliding the over 18's barrier back.

She had glowing reddish hair, red fingernails and a cherry coloured dress. She attempted to pull him away from the machine at a trice; first tugging at his jacket and then caressing his neck, whispering something in his ear. He shrugged her back. Her face, perfectly contoured as if created in clay, fired in the ovens of the hearts of man. Any man would spin at the shape of her lips. A big win for almost everyone. The gambler thought differently.

"Just piss off out. Go to *M&S.* You're ruining my concentration." He jabbed his arms towards her body and she left reeling. Her complexion matched her hair colour. She sheepishly walked to the back of the *McDonalds* queue. A lot of people in the service station had noticed their reverberating issue (the Chinese pair in *WH Smiths* were unaware – still reading Clarkson).

I glanced down the fast food queue.

Baz had slid in alongside Bell much to the disgust of the teenage bearded goth-like hippy directly behind him. Baz was aware of the piercing eyes (and pierced eyebrow) jousting the back of his head.

Baz beckoned us all closer. Chinny, Lee, myself, even one of the Chinese contingent who had strayed nearby.

"Don't worry mate," Baz said turning to speak to the large black coat with a pale studded man inside it,

"They're not pushing in. I'm just getting their food." Baz winked at us. "Right, *Big Mac* large meals all round? *Coke?* I won't remember specifics. I'm not doing it out of generosity. Just annoy the bloke behind."

"Baz, you seen the *big macs* on her," Bell said far too loudly, nodding towards the girl serving.

"You sure this is not *Burger King?* They look like whoppers mate," Baz replied even louder.

Bell and Baz continued to comment about the attributes of her combo hot cakes as the queue diminished. The bloke behind had left the queue, gone to one of those wall standing machines and was now already collecting his food, occasionally glancing back at Baz and talking to himself, slightly smirking. Baz hadn't noticed. He had one thing on his mind. Two things actually. *Double McFlurries.*

Baz was next in line. Hypnotised by her golden arches.

"Good morning. What can I get you?" she asked as Baz stumbled over. Baz wasn't listening. He didn't see her smile.

"Sorry?" he said, his body moving but his head fixed.

"What would you like?"

"I'd like to slap your tits with my meat," Baz said. She took a step back. "Sorry, sorry. I didn't mean to say that. I just thought it. Shit I mean, I didn't think it. I just said it. I'm so sorry. So sorry. Just forget that. It didn't happen. I've got special needs.   Can I have five happy meals? All with burgers, fries and 1% low fat milk jugs. Shit, done it again. Sorry. Five happy meals. Thanks."

He was escorted out. I ordered the food. I got a happy meal for Baz.

'Twenty two minutes' the driver had said. With two minutes to spare, we were all walking out of the services, declining AA roadside assistance again; bits of beef burger hanging from Bell's mouth, fries falling to the floor. Our

Chinese friends strolled in from the left; Alexa and Khan joined from the right. *The Red Arrows* would have been impressed with our formation. We were just missing the red and blue smoke (there was enough white smoke in the vicinity: cigarette smokers gasping, coughing and fogging our view; cloud creating vapers causing visibility issues at the local airport).

The mist cleared. A white van approached cutting through a gap in the parking spaces, beeping furiously at a loud loutish group of non-league football supporters who were not aware of pavement etiquette, deciding to bundle out of their bus and meander up the middle of the road. A group of cats that become tigers every Saturday when packed together. At least they are supporting their local team - gory hunters instead of glory hunters. And they had a bus.

Our driver swerved to avoid them, beeped again, and signalled the number 2 at them (even though there were about 20 of them, not 2).

I don't think I was the only one who thought our driver must be a revolving door of a character; a savage barbarian of a family man, bravely dribbling through a mob of studs up tacklers whilst cutting in from the wing to pick us up from the front doors. Aggressive but considerate. Jekyll and Hyde as Robert Louis would say. Naughty but nice as Salman Rushdie would advertise. Don't get in his way as the green cross code man would advise.

Then he accelerated, passed us, accelerated further with increasing celerity, clashed and crashed over a speed bump and turned the corner towards the motorway slipway. Probably never to be seen again.

"Fuck! That's £200 down the autobahn," Khan lamented.

"You gave him £200 for a taxi ride in the back of a van?" Chinny said astonished.

"I was in the front. You were in the back. Why do you think he pointed at me and Alexa to ride shotgun Bell? Pay the money and get VIP first class travel."

"I'd have given him £250 and bought the bloody van," Baz suggested.

We couldn't quite believe what we'd seen. How did he miss those sodding mindless football fans? Or rather, why did he just go? Drive past us? Not stop? Not pick us up? Not even wave goodbye?

We couldn't believe it.

Luckily Lee had filmed the lot and we all sat on a wall and watched it back. The Chinese managed to sneak forward and get front row seats. They laughed, said a few words to each other (probably something like, 'We are in England. Now we can buy a can of Nigerian chicken from a Romanian store where the shop assistant speaks Slovak but they don't accept Scottish banknotes'); they shook our hands, said goodbyes, bowed and went back in to the services. Probably never to be seen again.

I noticed they went straight back to the Jeremy Clarkson bookshelf.

We sat, ensconced on the wall.

No alarm clock (didn't work), No Steve Stevenson (Nazi had dropped out), No bus (?), No driver (gone), No Chinese (vanished into refugee status) – what else could possibly go wrong?

"Bitch!" Baz shouted. "She's only gone and not given me a happy meal toy!"

10

☑ University Reunion

☑ Road Trip

☒ Stag Party   ☑ Celebrating buying new camera

☑ 50th birthday

☑ New Job

☑ Just here for the beer

☑ 18th birthday

☒ Welcome to the UK ceremony x6

☒ Delivering goods to make money for his family

Alexa had gone back into the services to buy some more healthy food; this time honeydew melon, smothered in plastic and packaged in transparent cling film ready to choke the oceans.

Bell welcomed Alexa back: " You know honeydew is just mega sugary sticky liquid that's secreted by insects? So, you are actually........just eating insect poo.........on fruit basically."

Honeydew is one of those compound words. I can't say it without thinking of honey....or for that matter, without thinking of dew. Probably best I think of honey rather than aphids crapping all over the next 'one of my five a day'. Our very own doughnut, dingbat, drumstick bulldozed on:

"But if you want to eat insect poo, that's up to you." Alexa put the packet and half the contents in the bin. Landfill awaits.

"Eh, Bell, your grandad was a fighter pilot wasn't he? Can he not charter a plane and come and pick us up?" Baz shouted over.

Bell glanced down. "No mate. Went into Germany 1940."

Baz looked embarrassed. "Sorry Bell. Didn't realise. Was joking. I wouldn't have said it if I'd known he'd died in the war."

"Died in the war? No mate. He's on a beer-fest weekend in Bavaria. Plane landed in Munich last night at 19:40 – twenty to eight pm."

We were ready to give up. The smell of defeat, the taste of despair – a side dish to all those fries. Khan had fashioned a chariot for us before so could he do it again? We were fenced in by cars. Surely, we could rise up. Head north again. Time was diminishing. We needed a time machine. There was a man to my left, sat alone, sipping from a large coffee cup between talking on his phone. His name badge stated 'Dr Moreau'.

I heard him mention the final destination. This man was travelling to Coventry. A doctor. He's going to have a large car. Fake leather seats probably. If this doctor can take half of us, the other half can look for an optician. Or anyone. Someone. Anyone going to or near Coventry. We must get there before the night falls.

I was going to buzz myself over as his next patient, make contact. I was distracted. Another man shouting. My attention was drawn back to the front of the service station.

The stranger came early on, just after twelve, one Summer day through the biting wind and driving snow.

She wasn't *invisible.* She wasn't a *man.*

The lady with the bouncing red hair from the fruit machine area was walking at a rate straight across the road. Her heels denting the road surface. The man she was with earlier was following. His objections were audible.

"I don't need you anymore. Just bugger off. Yeah, that's it. Keep walking and say nothing." Her demeanour remained dignified and silent, vermillion but fully aware of the vermin's cutting words and equally aware that the whole of the car park was watching. Uncomfortable day time television. More DV than TV.

"That's it. Clear off. I never bloody loved you anyway. I'm not having you telling me what to do," his bellow tailgating her.

She leaned against her car door. Sealed lips.

He agitated further: "If I want to waste my money and lose it all in a fruit machine, I will."

She closed her eyes, dipped her headlights.

He threw the car keys on the bonnet. Put his fist down on the wing mirror cracking it a little and grabbed her hair.

Bell, Baz, Chinny, Lee, Khan, myself and even Alexa all stood instinctively without any of us knowing the others were going to do it. In the act of standing up, we all shouted 'whoaaa' or 'Oi' or 'stop' or NO' – we weren't so together with our words but it worked. He let go of her hair and hit her with his words instead.

"I've been sleeping with your cousin for weeks. She doesn't think I've got a gambling problem." He stormed away.

He was no longer in her life. A pleasing gearshift. I think it was her that had now won the jackpot.

Alexa went over to the lady and offered her a tissue. Her eye make-up was cascading along her cheeks. We stayed a distance away but moved off the road. My cunning plan, the lift idea from the saviour liberator medicine man who could blue light us to Coventry appeared again. Dr Moreau drove past........on his motorbike.

A couple of moments later, Alexa came back over to us.

"She's ok. Bit shaken up but she's grateful to you lot. Her name's Zivahno by the way."

"What sort of name is that?" Bell asked.

"It's Slov   Slov   Slovenian or Slovakian."

Zivahno looked up from the side of her car, put her hand up towards us all. She'd win anyone the QP.

"Can I just check?" Alexa asked. "Have you all been drinking?"

"Yeah, loads," said Baz. "Beer, vodka,   we got some left if she wants some."

Alexa ignored that comment.

"It's just she can't drive but she's heading north and she'd let us all get in with her."

I looked again at her car. It was a seven-seater, long, tantalising and majestic. A car that looked welcoming, inviting, alive. A large boot extending back. I lifted my head to peep inside. Real leather seats. A dashboard that screamed the words 'automated luxury'.

"But we need a driver." Alexa put the brakes on.

"No problem," Bell said handing a bottle of beer to Baz. "I've soaked it up with that burger," he continued. Alexa held her fury and Bell reversed up: "I'm only joking. I never drink and drive. There's only one liquid getting spilt when I'm in the back seat of a car."

"I haven't been drinking," said Lee in a flash bringing some urgent decency to the emerging emergency.

"I didn't think you could drive," Baz said.

"Took my test last month," Lee said with an instamatic reply.

"Perfect. Let's go."

Lee placed his camera in his bag. The first time I'd seen him detached from his high-resolution apparatus. His hand almost remained in a cupped holding camera position. Zivahno offered to hold Lee's camera so footage of the journey could continue. Lee seemed pleased. His smile was wide angled.

Seven of us. Seven-seater. Plus Zivahno as Snow-White with a shade of cherry red. Not the perfect fairy story after all. Eight doesn't go into seven.

Eight people scratching their heads. Sixteen eyes darting around. Seventy toes tapping.

One car waiting.

All bar one brain whirring. Bell took his hand off his chin and exclaimed, "I've got it."

Before he spoke, I had a vision of a large oafish centre half that could only head a ball, stepping forward to take the all decisive penalty to send us to the cup final in Coventry.......and then when he spoke, my excitement, my expectations, my hopes.........got ballooned over the bar.

Bell as a brush.

Bell as two short planks.

Bell and Beller.

When he said 'I've got it', why did I even bother listening to a man who cushions the underlay of his house by gluing piles of free carpet samples together in patchwork?

"There's one more of us than there's seats," he pronounced. Our anticipation extinguished. Then he spoke again: "But we've got one big boot. Chinny and his two cases in the boot. Rest of us in seats."

His looping over the bar penalty had become a rugby drop goal. Clever bloke. Before Chinny could object, he was lying in the boot squashed between his two cases like a soon to be born baby during the third trimester; and we were all seat belted up. Lee, literally in the driving seat. A man who knew how to drive a video camera. Not one drop of alcohol within. He'd just taken his test. Feet on pedals. Fingers checking wipers, lights, horn. Looking in mirrors. Hand on gear stick.

"There's no where to put it in."

"Steady on Lee. She just wants you to drive the car," Baz said.

"Ha, ha. Original," I said. "It's probably a push button start." Zivahno took his finger and guided it towards the button.

Lee remained focused.

I didn't.

"Right, everyone ready? Coventry   here we come."

Lee pressed the button. The engine disagreed with him, roaring in opposition. He hit the accelerator with both feet and we shot forward..........and we kept going.......and going. My neck shot back imprinting itself on the headrest. It felt like nought to sixty in three zeptoseconds.

Baz screamed nervously.

Bell screamed approvingly.

A corner was approaching. We could all see it. We didn't take it. Ziv's car collided with and pummelled a single road sign, lashing itself into pieces which rained metal down upon us in one fell swoop. Battered and beaten up, this car had lost the 'luxury' description. Belted about but we'd all belted up. Clunk Click. Everyone looked undead. The car was spitting blood. The sign was split into two, gnawed into a monstrous carbuncle, already rusting and carved by the car. One for '*Trav*' and another for '*ellodge*' with a third of the car wedged between them. The damaging scene enhanced by rubble either side.

"Fucking 'ell Lee. I thought you said you'd done your driving test?"

"Yes, I have but I never said I passed it.

Failed the emergency stop.

Re-take in three months."

11

☑ University Reunion

☑ Road Trip

☒ Stag Party   ☑ Driving Test ~~Celebration~~

☑ 50th birthday

☑ New Job

☑ Just here for the beer

☑ 18th birthday

☒ Welcome to the UK ceremony x6

☒ Delivering goods to make money for his family

☑ Divorce Party

Bell was first to exit the car. He'd squirrelled away a decaying couple of fries within his mouth. He would have made less noise chewing *Brighton Rock*.

Bell knew before he had been in the services three hours that Lee had not meant to murder him.

The car had been ripped open. Crumpled metal. Steam rising and visions of Coventry fading. Khan stepped out, reaching for Alexa and pulling her a distance away from the mangled tin. I'm not sure who got out next but within seconds, Ziv, Baz, Lee and myself were all standing alongside Khan and Alexa looking with intent at the crushed front of the car. The front bumper was a stamped upon apple. Unrecognisable. The rear was still intact. A trickle of oil streamed towards a nearby gutter.

"Is it still driveable?" Baz asked circumventing the remains.

"Steering wheel twisted. Front wheels both buckled up. Engine completely squashed in. Lights caved.

Windscreen cracked. One wing mirror hanging off. The other wing mirror parachuted to the floor. I'd say YES Baz, very driveable you fuckin' dipstick   but   I don't think the sat nav is working anymore   so we better walk it."

"Don't take the piss," Baz chirped back. "I know it's a wreck but can we like get it sorted?"

"Man, it's now an *airfix* model scaled 1 to 48 with some parts missing from the box. Most of us can't even change a battery. It's a write-off. Even scrap merchants will probably decline it."

"It's insured. If you guys can push it into one of those spaces. I'll ask my uncle to hitch it back," Ziv said.

It was the first time we'd heard Zivahno speak. Not one mm of Slovenian or Slovakian or even SloAustralian or SloAnyForeign accent within her.

"Alexa said you were Slov—", I took a punt, "Slovenian."

"Yes, my name is of Slovenian origin and my grandfather was from Maribor. He emigrated here, married my grandmother and both my parents were born in Britain. So was I. My middle name is Penelope."

I don't think I'd heard someone so typically English, a voice straight off *Radio 4*, a sweet mellifluous tone that soothed our jarred bodies.

Baz saw the chance to connect with a vivacious, vulnerable woman, recently disconnected from her partner and no longer emotionally attached to her car. Opportunity Knocks.

"I'm mixed race too. My dad was white. My mum was black. Well, they still are," he fumbled. "He's still white, especially his legs which have been banned from wearing shorts for years. My mum's still black. Decided against the Michael Jackson inspired beauty treatment." Baz paused to take a breath. Ziv smiled. Genuinely found it funny or pity or unable to comprehend his garbled attempts at conversation. Doesn't matter. If she liked him now, then she'd soon grow to dislike him. Most women do.

Baz couldn't stop talking. Nervous flirting.

"This might not apply to you, like being half Slovenian half British but me being proper mixed race, I get bloody annoyed that people think I'm black. I mean, I'm proud to be black but I'm proud to be white too. I'm half and half. Both. I'm as much one as the other." No pausing for breath – he continued. "When someone on the *BBC* (and I mean the telly news, not the Big Black C...   , um, yeah you know) says it's crying shame that only one black person has been nominated for a *Bafta* or an *Oscar* and four white people have, so what? Best people get nominated I say. I don't hear the same people moaning about Arsenal FC being discriminatory because most of their starting line-up last month was black. Unfair on the subs who were white? No, pick the best players I say." He blew out air instead of inhaling. "*Mobo's* started off all this positive discrimination. There's no Mowo's are there?" Ziv looked perplexed. "*Mobo*   Black Music awards. There's no prizes for white music. That would be racist."

"But Ed Sheeran and Justine Timberlake have won a *MOBO* Baz," Bell said.

Baz looked perplexed. "No, get lost. Have they? Probably token winner. And there's no white police in the Black Police association. But if the white coppers wanted their own exclusive club, they'd call it the KKK. Eff U Cee KKK I say. World's gone barmy."

Ziv was looking awkward, not knowing whether to raise her eyebrows or laugh.

Baz had made his point but just in case he hadn't attracted Ziv enough, he added a bit extra. "I'm mixed race so I'm as much white as I am black; as much black as I am white. I know I am going to be dead soon, another number on the annual cancer list. I'll just be dead. Dead data. I won't be on the news bulletin. No news reader is going to say it's unfair because not enough mixed-race people are dying of cancer." Baz started to mimic a news readers voice: "There's five deaths of cancer today and they're all white. More ethnic minorities need to be on the list of nominated fatalities. Unfair and discriminatory." He returned to his normal voice: "No, not going to happen."

Baz sure did know how to woo a woman.

Ziv nodded towards him, then proceeded to seek out Alexa and chat to her. Baz lit up his phone.

"Right, let's find a train station. Must be a train line nearby. Straight there. Fast. Direct. Quick. Qualified drivers. Driving test passed." Baz knew what he wanted.

Of course, every service station has got it's own train station these days. And airport. Helipad. Rocket launch, underground and barge canal. Parking limited to two hours though - plus a stand selling *ipad* and phone cases to people as you come out of the toilets.

"Found it," Baz shouted holding his phone aloft. A medal or a sign towards the heavens for help. "Acton Train Station. I've pinned it. About 1k over those fields. Piece of cake."

Fruit cake I thought. But it was the best idea because it was the only idea.

Baz started walking, mapping the route with his phone. Khan followed; Alexa seemed reluctant but she huffed a little and sauntered after her dad. Ziv took off her heels holding them both with just one finger via the straps. Her red fingernails and red heels becoming one.

Her legs were magnetic encouraging the rest of us to follow. Baz half turned as Lee, Bell and myself polarised ourselves behind Ziv. Baz was unaware that our fellowship of the King was not down to him. We were clamouring towards her Slovenian glamour; tactical delay, just enough to be beyond her 'sweet as a plum' bottom. We followed a beacon of red (red heels, red nails, red hair, red lips and a flowing cherry dress – everything was illuminated) and we were ready: ready to travel horseback across the fields and joust for this maiden's glove. She is Premiership. A few leagues above us. Cup Giant killers. Ensnaring Ziv would be harder than capturing the Cretan Bull.

We were slowing through the long grass, under broken hedges and over barbed wire fencing. Baz was adamant to go direct as his phone insisted, as the crow flies but we were trampling more like a penguin, waddling, pausing at every hill. One kilometre it certainly wasn't. Through cow pat infested fields, under damaged fences and over rusting gates. Michael Rosen's wonderful book came to mind and the hum of the words kept me going - along with Ziv's rouge colours. The thought of Bell on the dancefloor in Coventry 'catching a big one' was also motivating. Bell and a big one. Two wrestlers, Giant Haystacks and Shirley Crabtree, boogieing as a tag team, doing a full nelson slam till they clothesline each other. The DJ would give up in submission.

Baz, still a few yards ahead of the chasing pack stopped. "Halt", he shouted. "Go back." I now know why ordinance survey maps still sell. Baz's phone didn't tip him off regarding the marshland. A wet Dickensian bog. We were safe, circulating the edge but our scout now realised what mysophobia was. His little legs submerged up to the calves and neither able to shift forwards or backwards. Potentially dangerous. Hilarious.

Lee had his camera rolling. Unfortunately, Baz remained upstanding, the marshland refusing to take him down and he reversed his steps. Baz had got out but it gave us great joy to witness his footwear remain. Not one but both of his two ballerina size 8 shoes (laceless) were there, implanted for archaeologists of the future to discover.

Baz, on drier land but endangered by the steaming patties of cows, risked all to remove his socks, wringing each one out and return the soggy stripes to his Stone age man feet. He ignored the variety of jokes, a shoe box full of lampooning comments and we were off on a Roman foot march again. Baz, out in front, storming ahead, chorkling through the undergrowth; only hesitating when a thistle or bramble was trod on.

The thistle was going to be the least of his worries. Baz shouted, "We're about there. Over this fence and it's here somewhere. Phone says Acton Train Station."

The waste land looked rural, nothing resembling a train station, let alone Thomas' Island of Sodor. Baz vaulted the fence and started running across the barren ground which was more mud and worn away grass than nature. He stopped to turn around and shout, holding his hands around his mouth to aim his words further.

"I'll run on and hold the train just in case."

The rest of us had wambled to the fence. We lined up like the bottom row of a tin-can alley.

Baz shouted, "A caterpillar makes quicker tracks than you lot. Come on," and he turned.

Fortunately, Alexa and Ziv had glanced down to get their footing on the lower rung of the fence. The rest of us observed the massacre.

Baz was pummelled on the lower leg first. Subsequent gun shots echoed across the valley. Young men with guns firing at each other from either side of the stationary tanks and mad made barricade within the open ground. Baz caught in the crossfire.

Two burly men, completely camouflaged, came out of trees a further 30 or so metres beyond Baz and seemed to hold up flags. But it was too late for Baz. He was being hit all over this body, peppered with high velocity shots from his bare feet to his chest area. He finally hit the ground almost in slow motion and the two burly men ran across to him. One had what looked like a crown on his head and a large branch in his hand. The other carried a flag. Both had daunting magazine-fed firearms.

"Ceasefire," they shouted. "Hold fire." About 12 men, all in green outfits, boots and full head gear walked towards him, guns lowered.

Baz wasn't moving. His body littered in red. His legs a mix of blue and red. His feet were the colour purple.

I noticed one of the burly men lower his flag and kneel down next to Baz's decaying body.

"It's ok. None of the paint has gone in or near his eyes."

They slowly helped Baz up and signalled for us to come over.

"Don't worry," the man said reassuringly. "All the paintball guns have been locked."

Baz was quiet.

"I thought I was dead. I saw the red; thought it was blood and thought you were killing me. Then I saw my legs bleed blue and I really freaked out."

"You'll be fine. A few bruises tomorrow. Why are you here?"

"We're looking for this place." Baz directed the man to his phone screen, pointing at the map.

"Yeah, this is it. You're here." The man said.

"No, it's a train station. This can't be it. Acton Train Station."

"I'd read that again if I was you   and scroll across further. It says *Action Training Station – Paintball Stockade Limited.*"

"You absolute idiot Baz," Khan said shaking his head. "You must have pigmented liquid for common sense."

"That's quite funny actually Khan," Baz acknowledged, wiping his forehead and finding an almost tri-colour palette within his hair.

"That's not your usual kind of joke Khan," I chipped in. "That's the sort of joke Chi---". I hesitated. Diverting my head, I looked around and almost squealed: "Chinny. He's still in the boot of the car."

"Shitttt. And so is the vodka!" Bell added.

12

☑ University Reunion

☑ Road Trip (and painting experience!)

☒ Stag Party   ☑ Driving Test ~~Celebration~~

☑ 50th birthday

☑ New Job

☑ Just here for the beer

☑ 18th birthday

☒ Welcome to the UK ceremony x6

☒ Delivering goods to make money for his family

☑ Divorce Party

The burly men with the flags gave us mugs of tea and custard creams. No biscuit choice (a *jammie dodger* might have suited) but it was much needed refreshment. Baz got some vouchers and a couple of wet wipes plus they made him (not at gun point) sign a disclaimer form.

I held the tea in both hands, warming my fingers first but the heat soon found it's way throughout my body.

I decided to phone the Chinny mobile phone straight away.

No answer.

"Good news," I said. "It rang but he's not answering."

"Why's that good news?" Khan asked.

"Bloody obvious I should think," Bell retorted. "Phone's not crushed. Better chance Chinny's intact."

Khan took a long sip of tea. The effort of replying would have been higher than the reward.

Baz threw over a comment, giving the burly men their pen back, "He'll be fine."

"Keep the pen," they said. "You deserve it."

I read the pen slogan. It read: '*I shoot paint at ATS*' with the website printed on the rotation of it.

We shook hands, thanked them for the tea and I considered their colour scheme for my kitchen. We ambled towards the main entrance, through a car park of jeeps that were surrounded by puddle filled road holes and signs advertising the paintball experience.

What an experience we experienced. See your best mate in a war with a pack of gun frenzied *Dulux* dogs, drink tea and a free pen cach. Yes, they gave us all a pen as Khan gushed with the penultimate sound of an orgasm when he saw Baz's 'compensation' and was reluctant to explain his sarcasm due to the size of the gift givers: burly.

Waiting by the gates of *Action Training Station*, not a single train in sight. The sign opposite said, '*The Crow Road*'. No trains, no planes, no crows. Not one house either. Plenty of buildings behind us scattered within the trees but they consisted of an imitation half battered French bar, a wooden church front and a smattering of cardboard pill boxes dotted with paint. Wendy houses for grown men.

Khan was aware of the new challenge: "Don't bother getting your thumbs out. We could be waiting here for hours before civilisation finds us. There won't be any cars passing by anytime soon."

Baz got his phone out.

"No," everyone shouted.

It was going to be a long afternoon. Like watching paint dry. We were actually going to watch Baz's paint splattered body and dyed hair dry out. We needed something to keep our minds from going inactive. Instead, Bell started talking:

"I'm not a fan of guns. You read any American book or watch any American movie and there's guns."

I don't remember too many AK-47's flowing down the Mississippi in *The Adventures of Tom Sawyer* but Bell had a point – *Catch 22, Blood Meridian* and *To Kill A Mockingbird* all deal with serious issues whilst there's a hell of a lot of killing and slaughter in *Charlotte's Web*.

"Guns, guns, guns. I don't like them. But in the book I'm writing...."

Bell was writing a book? He'd only just learned how to colour one in.

"......Yeah, in my book, the council round up all the paedophiles, drug dealers, murderers, rapists and real bad criminals, and because all the prisons are full and overflowing, the government buy an island like Anglesey, relocating the Anglesey-ers, and put all these good for the death penalty crims on the island. Bit like a golden ticket for all the evil criminals but Anglesey ain't no chocolate factory."

I quite liked the story but I doubted Bell would be able to spell that long name train station. He continued with the plot:

"The island gets closed off. No one can get on and the baddies can't get off. They all start killing each other, ripping each other apart as they're all on this island starving. Then, around the island there's towers and tunnels for a group of people who've been offended against to get their own justice. And they won't need a *Marauder's Map* to track the bastards down. It's like a new sport and it will be beamed live on TV. Be better viewing than snooker."

"Sounds too much like *The Hunger Games* mate."

"No, my book has a twist. It's based on a novel by a man named Lear." Bell winked. "I'm calling it '*Restorative*' or '*Restorative: unsocial union and mans dominion*' – took that bit out of a Robbie Burns poem."

"What's the twist then?" Khan asked and then kicked himself for delaying the end.

"Ah, yes, the twist is that all the human rights law-yers and civil liberties nut cases complain, so, we bring them in with the offenders. Chuck 'em on the island to-gether. Now, let's see them defend them after they've been raped, tortured and beaten to bits. Everyone kills each other. Justice for the indefensible. Justice for those that de-fend the indefensible. You'll all be in it. Bit of you in that character. Bit of you in this character. Bit extra from my im-agination and then the character evolves and adds a bit themselves. But I'll change the names. Best seller everywhere."

"Apart from Anglesey."

"I've got a strategy to sell it," Bell said. "Firstly, I'll publish it in Norway as every book there gets 1000 copies bought up by the government for their libraries. Then I'll get publicity by getting it in the record books by having one sentence with 824 words in it. I'd have a blank page straight after my story ends just in case the reader wants a different ending. And finally I'll use lots of these words – civility, fancying, ramshackle, cinnamon, inquest, murmurs, vanilla sex – I read a book by a bloke called Blatt all about common words in novels and those words are used a lot by big selling authors like Jane Austin, Agatha, Bradbury and EL James. Good enough for them, good enough for me."

I can't imagine 'vanilla sex' was used a great deal by Jane Austin.

"I'd have assumed you'd have been more of a factual writer than fiction Bell," Khan suggested. "You could write the next '*Joy of Sex*' book; maybe call it Joy Of Pizza after Sex."

"Nah, I'm all fiction. It's about the characters. Hannibal Lecter is fiction. Fagin, TinTin, Rhett Butler, Juliet, Moll Flanders, Bigwig all fiction. Ron Weasley is definitely fiction – no ginger kid can have two real friends."

"You had a poem published once didn't you Bell?" Khan remembered.

"Yeah, '*The Railway Track*', all about my cousin Jack, rest in peace young chap."

Bell's poem was from the heart; I kept it in my wallet, along with a photo of Sophie (of course).

I got out my wallet, unfolded the paper and read the poem again to myself:

The Railway Track by Bell Rice

It started off as a great morning

Tim. Dave, me and Jack

We got out the football

And went down near the railway track

When we waved at the trains

We didn't know Jack was waving goodbye

There were only two minutes left in our game

Jack was about to die

The ball went over the fence

"I'll get it" – Jack did shout

Well it couldn't be dangerous

There were no trains about

Jack looked both ways: left and right

And it was ok – he couldn't see a thing

He started humming the 'Match Of The Day' tune

That was the last song he ever did sing

He picked the ball up

Tim roared, Dave and me gave 3 cheers

Then Jack stepped on the line

750 volts, shock–horror and his mums tears

It started as a great morning

We all went down the railway track

Only Tim, Dave and me returned

Jack never ever came back

Always gets me. My stepbrother also died on a
railway track when he was just one years old. I re-folded the
poem and put it back in my pocket. I kept Sophie's photo
hidden away. Bell broke my fragility:

"I did one about Venice too:

The roads are moving in Venice,

The waters are flowing through,

The roads are moving in Venice,

The streets are a colour of blue."

He paused.

"Is that it?" I asked.

"Yeah, one verse. I only went there for the day."

"Was that during your gap year?"

"No. As soon as I graduated I took a year off touring the UK, having my photo taken next to funny rude place names. I climbed Brown Willy in Cornwall, had my hands full in Titty-Ho up north, showered a lot in Sandy Balls down south, got well drunk in Bladda in Scotland and spent a fair bit of time sitting down in Shitlington Crags. Did you know there's even a place called Bell-End in Worcestershire? I'm like a tree of knowledge me."

"Fucking bonsai tree," Khan said.

A noise distracted us.

From a short distance away, we heard a murmur, a coughing, spluttering, ill sounding lorry approaching. Or maybe a tank coming to finish Baz off with a few frightful pots of paint. As it grew closer, the croaking engine became more imprudent and desperate. A vintage tractor on last legs perhaps. It was slowing. The sound of nuts, bolts and spanners inside a washing machine. A cacophony of jarring, throaty sounds which were increasing in volume but decreasing in frequency. Whatever it was, we felt it would implode before it got to us, no matter how torpid it was. Then it arrived:

A bus! A ramshackle bus but still, a bus.

Sent from the heavens. Perhaps Chinny is dead and he's looking after us. A gagging, smoking, crying wreck coming towards us. It slowed further and gave out a loud belch, stopping right next to us.

The engine appeared to give up right at our freshly formed bus stop. The driver squeezed out of his seat; a ghostly looking elderly man whose wrinkle ridden face was partitioned by a gang of ear hairs bursting out. Cauliflowers sprouting on either side of his antiquities. This clapped out fellow went to school before 'history' was a subject. He tentatively leaned towards his stick and stepped down from the bus, a quarter of a step at a time.

"Afternoon chaps." The old man said. "Doesn't look too good does it?"

Or sound it.

It was the afternoon my grand motor exploded.

"Trouble is ol' boys, I need to get back on the frog and toad to get to the next town to pick up about a dozen females."

"We'll fix it," Bell beamed. "Let's give it a push lads."

A bus that died before our very own eyes is not going to be resuscitated with a push. Even Bell knew that.

"Thank you young man," the driver said as he deepened into thought, twisting the greying strands of his patchy beard that looked like it would soon tunnel up and make contact with his ever protruding nasal hair. His thinking was interrupted by Baz's heightened interest in the passengers.

"These females, twelve of them. Any more details?" Baz recognised the chances of winning the QP trophy had multiplied by 12.

"Well, I dropped them off about three hours ago for afternoon bingo. It's my wife, few of her friends, a couple of others from the home. Just six of them in total."

Baz's face drained. Desire extinguished. Baz couldn't be bothered to argue how 'about a dozen' suddenly becomes 'just six of them'.

"Thrush," the elderly gent said. Was he ejecting his rash as he prodded his own hand forward.

Baz, his head recoiling back, "Excuse me?"

"The name's Thrush, Basil Thrush," and he teetered from person to person shaking hands and repeating on each occasion (with a quivering handshake), 'the name's Thrush, Basil Thrush'.

By the time Alexa was shaking hands with Basil, no one was able to retain the incessant joy anymore. It bust out, splitting lips and most of us had to hold our stomachs. I had toothpaste on my top and pee running down my leg but hearing he wasn't telling Baz he had some kind of chicken choking rash was a relief.

Khan, not one to appreciate long term communication, attempted to change the algebraic equation. He'd noticed the destination indicator on the front of the bus.

"You've come a long way in that bus."

"Not really young man. Just about 35 miles. No bingo halls in our village."

"It's just that it says: '*The Woking 925*' bus."

"Oh, right, yeah. Well spotted. Old bus I bought from *Furby Buses*. I can't change the destination name. Still, not much else wrong with it. Nice old motor she was till today."

Baz, puzzled but intrigued, asked, "She? You give the bus a name, do you?"

"No, never done that old chap."

"I'd call her Dolly Parton," Bell stated.

Khan asked, "Why?"

"The destination route on the bus says 'Woking 925' – for me, that's the Dolly Parton bus."

They say every dog owner starts to resemble their dog. As Basil started to laugh at the Woking 9 to 5 remark, his laugh developed into a choking cough and within seconds, he was bending over, and we were all wondering who would pull the shortest straw and have to do mouth to mouth. He became his bus. Spanners, nuts, bolts and flem were all spinning inside him. One massive cough which reached to the depths of his stomach and he was upright, breathing and no undertaker had been called. Yet. Pity - might have had a big hearse to take us to Coventry.

Alexa had walked about 150 metres down the road and she was returning. No doubt in search of a solution.

"There's a layby round the corner," she said as Basil was still retrieving his breath. "Vehicles there but room for a bus if you want to push it there and get it off the road."

It kept us busy.

We helped Basil back into his carcass, pushing him up the steps. No time to fit a *Stena stairlift*. He laboured into the seat and we all rushed around the back of the bus, grabbing different parts, huddled together, hands and arms ready.

"One, two, three   push."

This thing. She. Dolly. Was heavy. No move in it. Her. We tried again.

"One, two, three   push."

No budge.

We heard Basil Thrush shout something from the driver cabin. I left the pit crew and rushed down to his little slide across window.

"Tell me when and I'll take the handbrake off," the old sod said. Before I could answer, he did; and Dolly was rolling. This girl could move. We'd made 150 metres in a few seconds. Mrs Parton careered over to the other side of the road as we pushed her around the corner. Basil's steering as good as his handbrake lifting.

We parked the old thing (the bus, not the driver), leaving it behind two other vehicles. A rust ridden bin lorry that could bin itself and a parked up for the weekend community mobile library.

The final effort was exhausting and nearly everyone reduced their posture to a tired curve, mouths ajar and chests beating in and out. Ziv's was particularly noticeable. Baz, or barefoot Baz as we'd started calling him had kept upright and vanished towards the front of the bus. He'd come back energised.

"I knew it," he said triumphant, holding aloft a set of keys. "Dipshit Doug. He lives next door to me. Nice bloke but as thick as a plank. Literally makes Bell look clever. Hence the name. He works as a mobile library driver and he once told me over a pint that not one library has the same driver so they put keys inside the wheel arch. Like the masons or M.I.6. Secret like. Anyway, we got ourselves a route to Coventry."

Basil Thrush was happy to drive us there on one condition:

"We'll have to pick up my wife and her 88 mates or my balls will be 22 little ducks ol' chaps," he said smiling.

Nothing to lose. Everything to gain. A way of getting to Coventry. Basil, a proper qualified driver (if he stays alive and kicking) and lots of reading material. We boarded the mobile library and a call came in.

"Roger here. I'm Ziv's uncle."

"Sssssssscccchhhh," I bellowed out holding the phone closer. "Go ahead. I can just about hear you."

"Tell her I've picked up her car. Right mess. Gearbox gone, radiator leaking and the intake stroke is not allowing air into the cylinder."

Why's he telling me about a car? I need to know about Chinny. Probably hasn't even found the poor bloke yet.

"The connecting rod isn't rotating and the crankshaft isn't converting. The piston head---"

"Forget the car." He took no notice. Fucks sake Uncle Rog. Your niece is so much more interesting. He was exhausting.

"The alternator needs replacing and the glove compartment isn't shutting tight."

"Ok, stop there. Umm, I've got all that. Car no good basically. Did you see anyone get out of the boot? Have you looked in the boot?"

"Oh yeah. Ed. Yeah. He's all good. In the garage stretching out. Having a coffee." Rog tried to divert back to the car conversation. I passed my phone to Ziv.

Chinny's alive.

13

☑ University Reunion

☑ Road Trip (and painting experience!)

☒ Stag Party   ☑ Driving Test ~~Celebration~~

☑ 50th birthday (and still alive)

☑ New Job

☑ Just here for the beer

☑ 18th birthday

☒ Welcome to the UK ceremony x6

☒ Delivering goods to make money for his family

☑ Divorce Party

☑ Belated retirement party

Basil grew younger with the sound of a fresh

sounding, vibrant, teenage mobile library. A youthful expression was etched across his lined face as he pressed down gently on the accelerator.

"I've seen that old bloke somewhere before. I'm sure of it," Bell said. No one really took any notice until Bell exploded: "I've got it. Hangman."

"What?"

"He looks just like the bloke on the front of *the Hangman* board game. Remember that? Look at him. Now take off 30 years and that looks just like the bloke on the game box."

There was a very slight resemblance. Take 30 years off Basil Thrush and he'll look like Basil Thrush, just maybe one or two fewer furrows delineating his features. And if you put 30 years on any man except Dorian Gray, he'll look like the bloke from *the Hangman* board game.

"I used to love board games," Bell said. "I wanted to be a board game once."

"Not *Mastermind* I bet," Khan quipped over.

"I used to dream about having a full-size contraption like that from *the mouse trap* game in my back garden or turn my house into a *snakes and ladders* game with slides and climbing frames. Or even have a game invented all about me."

"There is one. *The Game of Life*. It's based on you Bell. Go round changing careers, getting fired and acquiring lots of babies," Khan said.

"And my car's plastic," Bell added. "I had some weird dreams. All my mates longed to be the *Milk Tray* man skiing down a hill and leaving their calling card on the four poster bed of a ravishing brunette but I wanted to be inside a packet of *Fizz Wiz popping candy*."

For us all, a day that had started off sweatily had accelerated towards sour.

Basil, one *hand in glove*, was still getting to grips with the library on wheels, introducing the sole of his shoe to the speed increasing pedal sporadically.

"Just smack your foot down like in a *Hungry Hungry Hippos* game Basil," Baz suggested.

He did and we were away. But we were still far from Coventry and far from *The Madding Crowd*. Bingo girls with bingo wings to pick up first.

When Basil Thrush smiled, the corners of his mouth spread till they were within an unimportant distance of his furry ears.

The mobile library was huge. A war and peace. A desk for stamping books out, two levels of fiction, a general reference section, colourful seating, some drawers labelled 'periodicals' and a fake pot plant screwed into the floor. Thousands of books restrained by neatly cut string. Bolted down cushion seats throughout – each with a seat belt (probably as a precaution in case Lee has to drive it).

It was destiny. A bundle of men on the verge of ticking the same 50-59 box on the census as Basil did just a few decades ago.

A bookshelf of old mates who all studied literature together but paragraphed off in various directions, coming together now and ending up in the most commodious vehicle. I often feel as if I am swimming through novels, pausing to dance on particular pages. I lift certain authors up and I cannot put them down, flicking through their words until they've nothing more to show me.

It's natural for men to have a senior crush on popstars or film stars, or in the case of Bell, the woman down the chippy. I believe weather girls are also popular with the age bracket I drop into. Balmy.

But my perfect women are authors. I hold a goblet of lust and fire for JK Rowling who gets better with age (and money). But JK doesn't sound right. I just couldn't call her 'JK' as we're romancing our philosophers stone:

"JK, we can lie in the garden gazing at the Dog Star?

JK, shall we stay in and clean the oven with dragon blood?

JK, let's visit the Edinburgh Potmakers museum."

Instead, "Joanne, do you want to do that '*Duro*' spell on me again?" Sophie often does the '*imperio*' spell on me – it makes the target obey every command.

But I must prepare for rejection. If JK declined moi chamber de secrets, I'd invite Gail Honeyman or JoJo Moyes. Perhaps Abby Jimenez or Maxine Morrey or Suzanne Collins or the author with beautiful white teeth, Zadie Smith.......or I'll bat for Robert Galbraith maybe.

I was facing a dilemma: which two authors would be my book-end dates? JK was top of my reading list but before I could decide on a novella, my wife phoned: Sophie Olivia – I often think she should have been christened Sophie Olivia Sabrina. She's less Joanne Kathleen and more S.O.S. though you need the special armed services to storm her embassy and end her siege with two bottles of captive prosecco. Her first words were surprising:

"Suck you lent."

I thought she may have said 'hi' first but maybe she's been on an afternoon wine bender with 'da girls....hic hiccup'.

"Say that again Sophie."

"Suck   you   lent."

'Ok', I thought. It's only June but if she wants to book in a promised unadulterated bout of fellatio for Easter, then I'll sign the contract now. But I needed to check. Sophie normally gives up chocolate for lent; normally lasts till the next day when she sees a *Cadbury's Crème egg* in *Morrisions* but next year she finally wants me to be her *Werthers Original.*

"Oh yeah, that's fine Sophie. I can happily let you do that." Maybe I sounded too eager.

"What? Just listen."

Had I miss heard her? "Suck me during lent you said?"

"Uh?"

"You said 'suck you lent'?"

"Yes, do I need to water your cacti plants?"

"Oh shit, knew it was too good to be true. Umm. Succulents yes, give the three by the patio room about half a cup of water each and the rest by the fireplace, don't worry about for now."

'Suck you lent' I thought. More like 'arid, remote, dry' and conquered recently fewer times than Neil Armstrong landed on the moon.

"Ok, I've given them a jug each already. Just thought I'd check. Bye."

She was gone.

I looked up from my bright coloured seat. I was sat within the children's corner of the library on wheels. Basil (the driver) was deep in conversation with Baz (the Baz we knew, Baz King, party planner, reunion organiser, trench foot patient).

Lee shouted over from the *mystery genre* bookshelf:

"Baz has still got dashes and splats of paint on him hasn't he?" I nodded, pausing, transfixed by what the squirrel seemed to be doing in the woodland scene behind my seat. Let's just say the artist had inadvertently painted a large twig and two acorns between the squirrel's legs. Nuts.

Lee pointed at my top. "You've still got that cum looking toothpaste on your shirt."

I looked down straining at the stain.

"Do you want to borrow one of my spare tops?"

That would make Sophie happy. Send her a *whatsapp* of me in a mauve top. "Yeah, why not? What spare top have you got?"

"I've got about 20, maybe 25. That's all I've got in my bag. 20ish spare tops plus a spare camera battery."

"20ish? You doing a boot sale?" Lee was more *Rodney* than *Del Boy*. More *Baldrick* than *Blackadder*. More *Rain Man* than *Iron Man*.

I've heard it said you can only fold a piece of paper seven times – one of those urban myths I've never had the bother to prove or disprove. Lee emptied his *Tardis* of a bag (it wasn't just bigger on the inside – it was actually shaped like a *Tardis* – his autism he calls it); T-shirt after t-shirt, all perfectly folded (more than seven times), came out of his closet and were placed in a perfect row on the bookshelf labelled 'self-help books'.

It was like a museum of classic 70's and 80's memorabilia. Lee was the curator. *Bagpuss, Captain Caveman, Mr Benn, Hong Kong Phooey, Betamax* (with a mauve background), *Bullseye* with the slogan 'super, smashing, great', the *Atari 2600, Big Trak, Frankie says... Relax*, a *Funny Feet* ice cream on a stick (perfect for sockless Baz right now), the *Goodies* and an out of place 21ˢᵗ Century

Spongebob Squarepants. Evidence enough for an ASD diagnosis.

Then more: *Trumpton, Wagon Wheels, Sinclair ZX81,The Fonz,* a *Chopper* bike, *Weebles* (some toy I've never heard of), a shirt design just of Tom Baker's scarf, a t-shirt for each of the *Banana Splits* and a *Blakes 7* shirt. A carefully considered mobile wardrobe, *foodification* of cheese and pineapple on sticks – I felt like asking why he didn't have a 'cheese and pineapple on sticks' t-shirt but he'd only go online and order more vintage *sashion* (a mix of the words 'sad' and 'fashion' – don't try it in *Scrabble*).

Rooting through his shirts, Lee was hit by a sudden anger.

"Where's my *Captain Pugwash* one? I must have forgotten it when I went to swap it for the *Big Yellow Teapot* one which I then took out as I thought the yellow teapot was a bit childish."

I wanted the Chopper one as it looked alright but it had a suspicious stain on it that definitely wasn't toothpaste.

Instead I chose '*Drooper*', one of the *Banana Splits*. Lee approved. Lee is clearly mad about retro vintage stuff – actually, we can lose the words 'about retro vintage stuff'.

Our library on wheels pulled into a retail area, a town of huge cuboid buildings with concrete football pitch car parking in the middle. The cement garden. Reminiscent of a prison, a large flat building with an exercise yard in the core. I've been fortunate enough not to ever go to one. And I've only been to a prison once but that was to visit 'Dovetail', a distant cousin who'd got 'wrongly done for burglary' my mum said. He just happened to be caught walking out of a bungalow in the depths of the night clinking someone else's jewellery with a claw hammer and a pair of my auntie's black tights on his head. Circumstantial evidence (plus his fingerprints all over the bungalow). I can't remember his real name but 'Dovetail' is now doing well on the 'curved and wide', selling pharmaceutical products outside schools. He even works weekends in and around pubs and clubs.

Basil identified his target group. A large herd of large ladies with larger handbags than they largely needed.

'Bingo' he had said. A sumo wrestling club was more likely. Basil excitedly started flashing his headlights and beeping his horn, grabbing the attention of weary shoppers and an assembly of teenage skateboarders who all looked as if their GCSE results had just come back as 'underwater' – below 'C' level. I commented as such to the others only to be taught by Alexa that grades are now 9 to 1 but she glanced at them again and agreed.

Basil shouted, "Bingo. Bingo. Bingo," with a feverish volume. I thought Lee had given him another *Banana Splits* t-shirt at first. Then I saw the dozen (six to be exact) females waving their money back at Basil.

"I'm not going to win the QP trophy here boys," Baz said.

"Who has that?" Khan asked.

"Not me," said Bell, "but I often won the KM. I was a perennial winner."

The infamous QP and KM trophies started off on a small-scale basis. Chinny, Kurgan and Jenkins (two other lads from uni, mates of Chinny) went into town one Saturday morning, popped into a trophy shop and bought a silver greyhound on a wooden plinth, engraved it as '*The KM trophy*'. The King Ming – to be awarded to the person who 'pulls the most minging woman each Wednesday and Saturday night out. This was balanced by '*The QP Trophy*'. The Quality Pull – a gold cheerleader, again on a wooden plinth, to be given to the person that managed to get off with a stunning girl. The small-scale competition grew and just about every male from our year competed. It was amazing that it was kept secret. There was a lad with one dodgy ear called Denzil who devolved espionage, mistakenly informing a sapphic girl called Bianca. She was bi and blackmailed us into allowing her to compete for the trophies or she would blow the cover, tell the females and not even the 2nd year student called Deirdre from Scunthorpe that looked like Velma Dinkley from *Scooby-Doo* but with Shaggy's chin-whiskers would have fallen for it. *Zoinks!* So, another entrant into our twice weekly 'sport'. Never going to be in the *Olympics* is it?

Us lot being a bit of an ugly bunch of guys, more likely to be cast in a *Discworld* movie than appear in *Kays catalogue*, we rarely ascended to win the QP trophy. If anyone won that out of luck or because they'd offered excessive alcohol, you basically kept it for the term. However, newcomer Bi-Bianca turned the competition upside down – she won the QP more than the rest of us put together. The KM on the other hand was fiercely contested for, and anyone could end up with it presented on Thursday first lecture or Sunday afternoons whilst watching *Sky Sports.*

The KM trophy should have been given to '*See-through Simon*' for keeps. We should have glued it to the palm of his hand.

"Do you remember *See-through Simon*?" I asked.

"Too right we do. Simon Fubar -the bloke seen wanking-off behind his curtains," Bell said. Translucent curtains. Hence the name. "Thick bastard", Bell added.

"Apparently, he was knocking one off to pics of Lorraine Kelly in *Hello magazine.*"

"Uhhhhh? Lorraine Kelly? Sick bastard more like," Bell updated his definition.

Basil Thrush started reversing the mobile library up.

"I think Kurgan has both the QP and the KM trophies."

"Oh yeah, on the final night of uni, didn't he bed Sonya from environmental science?" Sonya from environmental science looked like Sonia from *Eastenders*. This won him the KM.

"He then popped out to the toilet on her floor......" No en-suites in our day. ".....and lost his way back, went into Hannah's from geology room." Hannah from geology looked like Anna Friel from *Brookside*. This won him the QP. Complete luck as previously noted. It being the last night, she thought 'what the 'ell, why not?' and Kurgan becomes a legend. Hannah from geology had the best pair of rocks on her – you could have hung your coat and jacket off her nipples.

Our current legend, Basil Thrush, stopped reversing and started waving furiously towards his wife. They all
waved back. If Basil could have done a handbrake turn, he
would have. Instead, he just applied the brake and became
ageless, almost bounding down the steps. Viagra or
adrenaline. I must try both.

We all exited the mobile library. Lee was last off as
he counted the bingo girls, added in us and subtracted from
the number of seats. "Eight spare seats," he told me relieved. "Don't worry, I'm on the spectrum. High function-
ing."

Basil embraced a woman. We assumed his wife.
Correct. Basil then hugged and kissed all the others. We assumed just friends of his wife. We don't know. Basil might
be in his 50's and just appearing an 80 something
octogenarian due to his eager beaver personality.

After whipple tickling the final bingo girl which
seemed to be even more affectionate than he was to the
other little women, Mr Thrush castigated himself:

"Sorry one and all. Let me introduce you to my new friends. They helped me with the bus. Hence, why I'm driving the library.

This is my wife Berol. Shall I?"

"Go on Basil, you know you want to," Berol prompted.

"I've got pet names for them all. I wasn't going to. But I will now Berol said it's ok. So, starting with my wife. She's known as BJ."

With immediate effect, every single one of us was diagnosed with *tourette's syndrome*. A chorus of loud, instinctive and bulging 'fucks' rang out. Our heads twitching and our throats gulping, especially when Khan pointed out she had very few teeth. Mr Thrush reassured us:

".....which is short for 'Big Jugs'. She's always had them but now they're more big vases as they stretch down to your knees don't they luv?"

"They do Basil luv. Elongated."

I thought of *Stretch Armstrong*.

Berol confirmed: "But you don't mind do you Basil? As soon as I met you all those many years ago, I knew we'd marry and I'd have thrush for the rest of my life."

Was old Basil and wifey BJ serious or were we part of some huge *Beadle's About Candid Camera* wind up? Basil continued. He was serious.

"This," pointing at a lady who was bulging with life and overflowing with excess kilograms, "is Tonka. I've known Tonka since I was little." That must have been a long long time ago. "Over here we have Dumper." Enormous fairground pink candyfloss hair and a dodgem car for a body. Hook-a-duck! "Next," a smiling juggernaut dressed in red and resembling a swollen post box, "is WL or Wide Load." Her head was huge, like a moose but without the antlers. A sniper's dream. "She's our very own Pamela Anderson. Used to be a lifeguard many moons ago. *Baywatch* aren't you luv?" *Baywatch*? Behemothic more like. "Next to her is Dusty. She's new to the group so I haven't thought up a name yet." Dusty was her real name? "But I will." I'd have thought her nickname was as easy as 3...2...1...Dusty Bin. "And finally, last but not least, one of my favourites   is Skinny Latte."

Skinny Latte was no slim chicken and could easily have been called any of the other names. We didn't ask why Skinny Latte was her name but Khan whispered to me that her tits probably taste of coffee but we'll never know......hopefully.

The chunky, lumpy, burpy group of *dirty gerties* lined up to greet us like Russian Dolls, each bingo girl just a bit shorter and wider than the *legs eleven* next to them.

Basil had already agreed to take us to Coventry before dropping the bingo girls off home later and they all agreed. They agreed even more when Khan suggested he run into the supermarket between the bowling alley and the bingo hall to trolley up some Dutch beer, French wine and Mexican tequila all courtesy of his American express. Tonka passed a £50 note to Khan, "We've had a small win on the bingo so we're out for the night."

"I am looking forward to some liquid," Baz said clinking an invisible glass. I knew Baz well. He was acting out a positive vibe. His internal doubts were outwardly resurfacing again.

"You alright mate?" I said as I half raised my invisible glass back.

"Yeah, you know   just   think too much some-times   upsets me   but at least I know. Everyone should know in advance. I can make the most of my life; my life that's left. Everyone should know when they're gonna die. Everyone else,   it just creeps up on them and then they're dead. Car accident, heart attack, bee sting, hit by a bus. Bang. But I know. I know I've got so long so I feel lucky I guess. Make most of it." I had to just nod. Baz kept talking: "I'm ok. My hope dies and then re-awakes. At least I'll go out at the top. Die of old age and it's the circle of life."

"What do you mean, circle of life?"

"Well, you're born, your bottom's wiped, you can't do much, no teeth, piss yourself, watch daytime TV. Then, decades later, you get too old and your bottom is wiped, you can't do stuff, no teeth, piss yourself, watch daytime TV. Only difference is when you're a baby your mouth is in a woman's bosom. Circle of life mate."

I nodded again. He didn't need my words. Or want them. His own words wanted to change the subject:

"Where's Khan got to? I'm getting thirsty." Waiting at this barren water hole, patient for Khan's rains to come, a stone hit the front of the library. Then another and another.

The wanton assault was coming from the clutch of filibusting skateboarders who were loitering outside the ten-pin bowling alley. They were a group of skittles with their hands pinned inside their trackie bottoms. I wanted to send a 16 pound bowling ball spinning towards them, striking all the maggots but their stone throwing attack had ceased and Tonka suggested it was best to ignore their attention seeking aggression.

One of the jackals, not on his skateboard but holding it, started walking over. More of a swagger with intent. A wobble of a walk that swayed from side to side. The remainder of his clan looked on from a distance.

Tonka again reminded us to remain within a peacekeeping policy.

"Dat wankd innit fam. Me brares sayin' yuse bunch o muppitts diss. Yuse lot is just a joke innit. Wots wiff the fuckin' whack spastic bus boi? Dats joke. U is proper Fuggerz, Blad."

"What did he say?" Lee asked.

"No idea but it's not pleasant." The advanced linguistic ability of six Chinese refugees who had just landed in our country compared to the deficiency in communication skills in evidence from this English young man was alarming. It's just so tough for some young people today. They have vandalised their own parks, the council have not provided them with enough blank walls to spray graffiti tags on, they even have to walk ten metres to their front gate before

169

the taxi picks them up to take them to the pupil referral unit; and there's 'nuffin' on tv. If they watch porn in class, they'll have their phone taken off them (temporarily). They have stamped on the youth club chalk so that's why they missed the shot, so they snap the pool cue. There's too long a waiting list for *Lego therapy.*

Their teachers have rudely asked them to write the date and actually do some work. The demands on them. There's not even *Multi-coloured Swap Shop* on TV on Saturday mornings anymore. And, can you believe it, when they beat someone up on the playground, they only get offered a hot chocolate drink in the *calm down rainbow room?*

Just awful for them. Traumatic. Children in post war Britain in the 40's and 50's just had it so easy. It's harsh on kids today – they aren't even allowed to play with conkers even if they managed to nick someone's bike, wheelie up the middle of the road, work out what a tree is and use their bb gun to shoot down some conkers; then learn how to tie a knot and play one handed whilst the other hands smokes a spliff.

170

To be fair, most young people these days are not like that but this dysfunctional, vulnerable, hooded, needy young person was. Out of order. For real. Endz.

"We was finking if dis girl....." He raised his hand to signify Alexa. "....wanted to hang out viv hus."

They wanted Alexa. We wouldn't have even handed over Tonka – Tonka, our very own Terry Waite, sustained a peace envoy role:

"No, she's alright over here thanks. We're just leaving."

"You wan sum instead do ya?" He spat on the floor and wobbled back (Lee said it was like a *weeble*) to his pugnacious nest.

Tonka remarked, "See, stay calm, be polite, ignore it and it will go away."

Bell added, "I'll try that with my next STD."

Tonka's strategy might have worked but the skateboarders were oppositional and defiant to a fair reasonable approach. They returned as a flagrant group, a menacing syndicate of *weebles* all swaggering out of synch. I wondered why they didn't skateboard over to us with them having the forethought of coming out with their mode of transport. I wondered what their drug of choice was. These young gentlemen weren't drinking *Top Deck* lemonade shandy. I wondered why they weren't all at home completing their 'citizenship and good character' homework project. I should wonder less.

The same skateboarder that spoke before stepped forward. The group clustered behind, some with two hands inside their pants; one of the skateboarders was filming it on his mobile. Lee returned fire with his camcorder.

"We woz finking bout ya motor."

"What about it?" Basil asked but he was verbally cut down.

"Shut it grandad. Fucenz *Papa Smurf* prick."

Tonka brought some much needed restraint to the increasing tension:

"Listen, young men, we don't want any trouble. That's all we ask."

I didn't want any trouble either. I did have a dislike over their poor use of language. I wanted to suggest they say 'we were thinking'. Getting *were was* correct and making sure they pronounced 'th' rather than 'f'. I decided against it as I'd already ignored their baggy trousers being three sizes too big. Madness.

We were all impressed with Tonka's negotiating skills. Calm, placid, measured, patient and composed.

The situation escalated.

"Hand over yers fones and cash." They waited. "I is no budging. We can smash that van of urs up."

"Come on lads," Tonka persisted. "Just head back. That's enough." Her eyes were suggesting that they need to understand each other.

"Fuckz you," the skateboarder said. "Yuse fink we donner mean it." He dinted a knife from the inside of his boot, almost slicing his own calf. "I gonna cut yous lot up."

Another skateboarder stepped forward with an incisive stride. "Money now. Phones."

The group all lifted knives of different sizes and serrations from their boots. Two were waving their weapons in the air. The rest were holding them upright and still. The blades looked cold. I glanced at Baz. He looked ill – they had knives (and they had footwear).

Tonka was done with negotiation:

"Listen you little shitty *milky bar* kids. We've 999'd this and....." We hadn't. "....and you can all bugger off yourselves. Now go."

In pre-21st century, when Tonka grew up, when 'naughty' teenagers were robbing glass lemonade bottles off doorsteps, pilfering *marathon* chocolate bars from gift shops and generally rankling for six whacks in the headteachers study like in '*Kes*', this approach may well have worked. Clip around the ear. Boot up the petulant backside. Sod off or I'll tell your parents. Unfortunately, we were up against a group whose skateboards were just there for a quick off road getaway before they smashed a car window, joy rided it, got cop chased, had their tyres stung by a police stinger, legged it on foot, surveillance helicopter sent out, appeared on *police interceptors* on *Channel 4* and then received a heavy modern criminal sentence such as three points on a license they haven't yet got, six hours community service (five of which they'll get let off as they're feeling a little 'under the weather') and the rest is suspended. A defence lawyer worth their weight in depressants will appeal, get them off scot-free and even manage a bit of compensation for the mental hardship they had to endure by being in a cell for 45 minutes without *4G* wi-fi.

This wasn't *Dukes of Hazard.* They meant it. Those knives were real. Even Bell was ready to hand over his cash. They could have my mobile no problem. They'd only throw it back. Not modern enough. Not worth getting a bus into town to pawn it. Plus, a couple of calls off Sophie would have been more punishment than was actually judicially fair anyway.

We were about to die.

We were about to be saved.

Khan returned, rattling his three trolleys full of liquid refreshment.

It wasn't Khan that saved us.

It wasn't the alcohol.

It wasn't even the trolleys.

He'd met our six Chinese friends in the 'ready meals' aisle. Chinese people looking for Chinese supermarket food – I knew *Sainsbury's 'taste the difference'* selection of takeaways was good.

All six stood in an arrow formation in full Kung-fu pose (it transpired later that only the man at the tip is a 4th Dan black belt master; the rest were acting in support and admitted to being more origami masters than any martial art but it looked right).

"Ha, ha. Clear off Chinkies. Go 'n get some prawn crackers. I got blade 'ere."

Our friend at the tip of the arrowhead launched into a revolving acrobatic leap, one leg kicking out to dislodge the knife, the next swinging round to slap the repellent teenager in the chest, throwing him back several metres. A fouetté followed by a landing in perfect pirouette – resemblance of a holly leaf landing over a stricken blade of grass. Our friend (*number one super guy*) then back flipped, smoothly lowering into a semi-kneeling position, one flat hand across the neck of the teenager, the other raised and about to swing down (*faster than the human eye*). Mash gets smashed.

The remainder of our friends in perfect symmetry held their poised position, all flat handed and appearing ready to launch. Vipers about to go at lesser snakes.

The Chinese man's hands, '*born from an egg on a mountain top*', purposely quivered above the head of the now not so tough teenybopper. *Monkey magic.*

Tonka shouted over to the teenagers behind, "Drop your weapons." They did. Her British negotiating skills reinforced by a Chinese threat of nuclear attack. International cooperation.

The scalp of the abhorrent less than super supercilious youth, sunken eyes full of fear and a voice empty of words, was lifted by our Mr Miyagi. "Now go," the Chinese man whispered.

The teenager got up and ran, almost in zig-zags, not knowing which hole to scamper in to. His baggy trousers were falling and needed him to hold them up whilst running. Next time he scarpers terror-stricken from the patron saint of mobile libraries, he'll buy some tighter fitting trackies.

14

☑ University Reunion

☑ Road Trip (and painting experience!)

☒ Stag Party   ☑ Driving Test ~~Celebration~~

☑ 50th birthday (and still alive)

☑ New Job

☑ Just here for the beer

☑ 18th birthday

☑ Big welcome to the UK ceremony x6

☒ Delivering goods to make money for his family

☑ Divorce Party

☑ Belated retirement party

☑ Jackpot win on the bingo x6

Incoming text.   Yeah,   her.

SOS: < I'm really happy emoji x2 happy face > 4.53pm

      One of those affirmation texts; a statement that is begging for a reply. The fishing line cast and she wants me to ask 'why?' or 'what's happened?' or 'Good, how come?'. I'll just ignore it. I could gamble on how long till the next text comes through but before Dumper, sat to my left or WL, sat to my right would have chance to ask the odds, her abutting text will be through. Sure enough:

SOS: < R U going to ask me Y emoji thoughtful face > 4.55pm

No question mark. Infuriating lack of punctuation - then it arrives but two of them!!

SOS: < ?? emoji sad face> 4.57pm

I replied:

< cakes on offer 1 for 2 found have you because happy are you > 4.59pm

SOS: < ??? emoji 2x sad face > 5.00pm

<boustrophedon> 5.00pm

SOS: < ..... & u wonder y u don't get sex emoji cucumber >
5.02pm

< sorry saggy > 5.03pm. Predictive text. Accidental. Should
have said 'Sophie' not 'saggy' – accidental yeah. I noticed
she was also *typing* at the same time.

<someone grabbed my phone and sent a stupid message.
No idea why. Why are you really happy? > 5.05pm.
Question mark included.

An instant response. SOS: < Don't bullshit me saying someone grabbed your phone. I know that was you emoji rage face
> 5.05pm

SOS: < I'm happy because I've just tried on some clothes.
Last tried on 20 years ago emoji 2x smiley face > 5.08pm

SOS: < and they still fit emoji thumbs up > 5.08pm

I desperately wanted to type back 'a scarf doesn't count' – my fingers were hovering over the keys....

< Wow. That's brilliant news. I can't wait to see > 5.11pm

I'd love to see her in something blue, long and flowing. Like a river.

< See you tomorrow > 5.12pm I added in the hope that would end this unhealthy 'text life'.

SOS: < Y haven't you done any excited little emojis emoji sad face > 5.12pm. No question mark either.

I'd never typed OMG. I just like proper full English words. I'll occasionally recede to typographical symbols – grawlixes such as $#&%@! but they're too 'primitive' for Sophie - OMG FFS 4COL TTFN. I know she's not the only cyber-slanger who talks in such a 'lettered' way as this texting 'language' I call Sophie's *Softheaded-speak.* There's not an emoji (or a grawlix) for absolute bewilderment....is there? I don't know.

< Battery fading. Can't text. Emoji battery > 5.15pm. I actually sent her an emoji.

I never know what emojis to send her. It's a nightmare enough coming up with Christmas gifts each year these days. Last year I bought her a leg waxing hair removal machine that she used as a facial hair trimmer, a charm for her *pandora* bracelet (they're too expensive so I just got one of those silver tokens out of a *Monopoly* game – she got the wheelbarrow. She didn't realise. She loves it. I think I'll get her the top hat next year), a chew toy from *Pets At Home* (we haven't got a dog) and a new phone which she chose herself. The phone was more expensive than the first house my parents bought.

She phones her parents on it every single day. Sometimes they accidentally answer. Yes, her mum and dad are eternally grateful to me for marrying her or 'taking her away' as her mum affectionately calls it. Her dad calls it 'removing the package'. It also saved them stacks of pounds each year with deliveries from *dunkin' donuts*. She's their only child - after she was born, they decided to stop whilst they still outnumbered her.

They quite often invite me round. Occasionally, they invite Sophie too. It's love but best served in low doses. You see, Sophie's mum suffered with morning sickness.....after Sophie was born. But yeah, they do love her. They proudly show me memorabilia of when she was younger: a *Polaroid* pic from her first birthday, a set of photos (still in the *Truprint* envelope) of her first day at school, a *Honey Monster* balaclava (free with six tokens cut out of *Sugar Puffs* cereal boxes) they used to put on her whenever they took her out in public, an old camcorder video of her clearing her plate at an 'all you eat' buffet, her birth certificate, her exam results, pupil of the week certificates, a letter from the school nurse saying she's overweight and almost obese – she was already seven stone back then – her excuse is that they fed her too much in pre-school that week.

Twelve more texts came through. Most were short and curt. One was an essay of abuse, a thesis of nuptial persecution which mauled my screen but was quickly forgotten. In real life, she's like my credit card – contactless. But I get a *get out of jail card* and I'm away for less than 12 hours and she bombards my phone with text after text. It was

Misery – a psychotic nurse was holding me virtual prisoner and torturing me. But Sophie's not a nurse. I bought her the 'outfit' about 25 years ago. It's still sealed and in the original packaging. It can stay there. *Ann Summers* doesn't do a Jaws, a Dementor or a Miss Trunchbull fancy dress.

Her thirteenth and final text (lucky for some; the 4 leaf cover emoji came to mind) said:

SOS: < when u get back, I think we should sleep in separate beds emoji x2 bed > 5.28pm

Fine with me I thought. I'll choose Heather, the single mum from over the road.

I've always thought she was a 'bit of alright' and she asked me if I'd mow her lawn once. Literally, not metaphorically. She's a tattooist at *Heather & Maurice's Inks* in the High Street.

A painted lady. She's patchworked in Celtic knots, geometric polygons, Japanese lotus flowers, gothic lettering, Maori motifs and a 'we live with the scars we choose' quote on the back of her neck.

185

One day, it's conceivable I'll set myself free, cross the road like *Frogger* and mow her lawn. Metaphorically, not literally. She'll just want me to have a tattoo. I wouldn't. Always been reluctant after a bloke from work (Luke) had to have a polo player picture and the word 'Ralph' inked next to a 'Lauren' he already had. His new girlfriend (Jayne) didn't like his ex-wife's name (Lauren) tattooed on his arm. Luke has never played polo. He also wears *Tommy Hilfiger.*

I forgot about Heather. Probably best to. She's from a known family of reprimands and delinquents. Her brothers didn't go to private school but they were always in small classes, had extra teachers and got lots of special trips to outward bound adventure centres – the hardship of exclusion and young offenders institutions.

Each December 31ˢᵗ, her family celebrates New Years' Eve without Heather – they rattle their bars, set fire to their cells, abuse the guards and see the new year in with the views from Wormwood Scrubs' roof garden. Christmas is a time for family they say and most of them are together.

Even Heather's mum is 'inside'. She broke into *Heather & Maurice's Inks* shop, nicked the tattoo gun and tortured someone she took a dislike to.

Heather, *The Tattooist* might be pleasing to every single one of my *207* bones but at least Sophie just bruises my humerus and her family don't break my legs.

Sat on the mobile library, I was a thorn between the roses of WL and Dumper. Plenty of nectar there. Mr Thrush was pedalling fast and we were making ground up.

The library rattles across the countryside keeping the head up and I kept myself to myself.

There would have been no opportunity to chat to Wide Load and Dumper even if I'd have wanted to.

Basil shouted to the rear of the library, "Drat. It's the police." We all looked behind. Basil looked in his mirrors again. The orange flashing light of the traffic police pulling us over. Basil indicated and slowed.

Our six Chinese friends back on board with us (they ended up at the bowling alley after getting a lift from the van driver. He didn't try to kill us after all. He'd just gone to get some petrol. '*Fuelish*' of us). They panicked, looking for secret doors within the bookshelves. They've been watching too much Agatha Christie and Inspector Morse on national Chinese state TV.

The darkness of the motorway dotted with lights from behind and in front added to our confusion. Our Chinese friends were in a perturbed fluster. Two officers exited their police vehicle and marched down the hard shoulder to the side of our library. They banged on the door adjacent to the driver. Ziv and Bell (finally travelling 'shotgun') opened the side doors.

"Uncle Rog," Ziv said open mouthed.

"......and Chinny," flapped Bell, firing his half-eaten chip-sticks against the dashboard.

15

☑ University Reunion

☑ Road Trip (and painting experience!)

☒ Stag Party ☑ Driving Test ~~Celebration~~

☑ 50th birthday (and still alive and back with us)

☑ New Job

☑ Just here for the beer

☑ 18th birthday

☑ Big welcome to the UK ceremony x6

☒ Delivering goods to make money for his family

☑ Divorce Party

☑ Belated retirement party

☑ Jackpot win on the bingo x6

Chinny, still morphsuited up though in need of a
costume change – a concoction of odours encompassing
oil, diesel fuel, vodka and Nooteboom sweat. Just one seat
left unbuckled on our mobile library now. We did offer it
to Uncle Rog but he said he'd try and catch up with us later
as he had another couple of jobs to do. Lots of traffic
equals lots of breakdowns equals lots of jobs equals loads-a-
money – *Bob's your uncle*....though he's not; Roger is. Big
thanks to Uncle Rog and his flashing orange light. He was
off and then we were off. He'd only stop when he gets to
his first breakdown. We only stopped when we hit traffic
and lots of it. I have a real *fear and loathing of las* traffic.

*We were somewhere on the edge of the M1 desert
when the traffic jams began to take hold.*

Basil Thrush was in the middle lane and refused
Baz's repetitive guidance to switch lanes. Other drivers were
unable to resist the capricious temptation of a gap in the
gliding traffic. They'd slip in, only to come to a standstill

and feel irascible as the lane they were just in started up and passed them with ease.

We came to a sudden stop. No lanes were moving ahead. No gaps leading into temptation. A helmet on two wheels weaved between caged vehicles and gambled with doors opening, filter eager drivers and panting canines gaping through windows. An harras of horses hurtling down the hard shoulder may have got us closer to our finishing post but galloping on *Shadowfax* or *Black Beauty* (Baz would have been on *My Little Pony*, bare feet in the stirrups) wouldn't exactly be safe either. Apparently, there are about 200 horses killed each year 'for fun' in UK horse racing. Humans being in-humane. Stakes for steaks. More than a butchered shambles but the 'sport' rides on. If Usain Bolt and 199 other sprinters got slaughtered every 12 months whilst doing the 100m, the sport would be for the high jump. But gridlocked on the main artery to Cov, there were other things for me to be pained about.......

I came across my traffic aversion, a triad of aberrant loathing:

To our right, a driver of a reasonably priced car but with a number plate unpersonably personalised. More of a wordsearch of jumbled letters than a proper plate.

If I win the *lottery*, I won't buy a personalised plate. If I win the *euro millions* and I'm *Brewsters Millions*, with so much, I'm not even able to flush it away, then I'll get her 5OPH1E. I could not turn all road users dyslexic by purchasing any cheap confusion like 409H13. Everyone's got a personalised plate these days and the driver to my left was no exception. He couldn't afford TE5T1CLE so he went for T3571CL3.

One vehicle in front, my next objection was evident. A sign on the back window that's becoming an infection. 'Young Person On Board'. My eyes glanced around the stalemate of traffic and I saw 'Dad's taxi', 'Baby On Board', 'Little Monkey on Board', 'Princess on Board', 'Baby in Car', even a 'Poodle on board' and 'this drivers so stupid they stick a diamond shaped sign in the back window that means nothing'.

What do they want me to do when I see their plethora of signs? Eh, the car in front has a sign that says 'Baby On Board'. I know, 'coz there's a baby on board, I won't ram into the back of the car......ah, too late, I was reading the sign and forgot to brake'.

Still, probably better than doing what every Morris Minor, Ford Cortina, Vauxhall Viva and other car did in the 70's and cover the back window with stickers of every holiday place you'd been to. The joy of being stuck in traffic and knowing the family in front had been to places like Skegness, Blackgang Chine, Powis Castle, Blackpool, West Midlands Safari Park, Torquay, Butlins Minehead, Lands End and Derwent Pencil Museum (I've never been there either).

To my right, the final prong in my forked triad of travel animosity and this one is so much worse: someone on the phone whilst driving. It doesn't really matter if someone has a 'Grumpy Old Man' sign in their back window even if it's next to a Cheddar Gorge sticker and above an impossible to comprehend number plate. But driving on the phone   NO.

Try walking a tightrope and texting.

Try feeding a lion whilst on your mobile.

Try making a call when you're about
to take the decisive penalty in a
World Cup final shootout.

No, you're not going to. It's either dangerous or you
need to concentrate or both. But put someone in charge of
120 stomping horses, a mangle of metal on four wheels and
they think it's perfectly safe to use a mobile phone. Rabid
dog and bone.

I know Khan thinks the same and for *two* good reasons. He'd also spotted the phone user to our right. Traffic
started to move again, just a couple of miles per hour, then
stop start to about ten, then five again. The traffic was
inflexible of a consistent speed.

At around 10mph, with the driver still talking on his
phone, Khan had depleted all patience. Banging on the side
window of our library, Khan started to shout, "get off,
you're driving." His sounds and window bangs should have

been clear. Khan was transparently loud and understanda-
bly in rage. The phone driver wasn't ignoring on purpose.
He had no idea we were now all trying to get his attention.
He was otherwise engaged. Bell had enough.

At 5mph, Bell checked for motorbikes, opened our
passenger door, jumped out and tapped on the surprised
driver's door.

"Sorry sir, can I borrow your phone by any chance.
We've got an emergency."

The man was taken aback and hesitated. His call
was more important than Bell's emergency and more important than the critical emergency ahead of him if he
keeps talking and driving.

Bell reiterated, "Emergency."

The man grudgingly handed the phone over.

"Thanks." With immediate and steadfast force, Bell
launched the phone beyond the hard shoulder and within a

javelin length of brambled trees and foliage, at the side of the motorway.

"Thanks again. Emergency over."

Traffic slowed further and we took the next exit deciding to go cross country. The call of the wild. I reminded myself of Hamlet - ~~Happiness is a cigar called............~~ Not that Hamlet, the other one: Happiness is going *country matters*. Alas, poor road users when there are mobiles about.

16

☑ University Reunion

☑ Road Trip (and painting experience!)

☒ Stag Party   ☑ Driving Test ~~Celebration~~

☑ 50th birthday   ☑ Thelma & Louise also back with us

☑ New Job

☑ Just here for the beer

☑ 18th birthday

☑ Big welcome to the UK ceremony x6

☒ Delivering goods to make money for his family

☑ Divorce Party

☑ Belated retirement party (phone now switched to off)

☑ Jackpot win on the bingo x6

We were collecting people. A *panini* sticker album on wheels. Did you know that there are over two million *Mills and Boon* books under the M6 toll motorway – they're meant to make the tarmac more absorbent?

But there's not one in our library. Tonka had just spilt a splash of vodka near her feet. At least, I hope it's a puddle formed from alcohol. I was going to test the absorbency of romantic literature but the nearest book to my eye (I'm still sat near the well-endowed squirrel in the children's section) is *Five Children and It*.

We've 20 people and It. Baz, Khan, Alexa, Lee (still filming), Chinny now in his Jesus outfit, myself, Ziv, Basil Thrush driving, Mrs Thrush (BJ), Tonka, Dumper, WL (Wide Load), Dusty (still no official nickname), Skinny Latte (coffee tits.....we guess) and six Chinese friends (names unknown but one could be a descendent of Bruce Lee).........plus.......'it' (Bell) and one spare seat.

The library was three miles from Coventry station, but before we'd rattled along for five minutes, Baz began to look out of the window and say, 'Aren't we there yet?'

I love the Nesbit 'It' book. I could not declare my vows to just one book. Double edged love. The feel of the books. The stories within. I have always been faithful to Sophie, on the shelf back home. But I have been unfaithful to all the books I've loved. I loved *Stig of the Dump*, the classic by Clive King. But then I fell in love with another book, then another.

I take you, *Fantastic Mr Fox*. I promise to be true to you in good times and in bad, in sickness and in health; I will love you and honour you all the days of my life.

But then, before long.......

I take you, *The Snowman* to have and to hold from this day forward; for better, for worse, for richer, for poorer, till death do us part.

I've loved so many:

Where the Wild Things Are, *Treasure Island,*

The True Story of the 3 Little Pigs, *Billy Liar,*

Paddington, *Lord of the Flies,* *Life of Pi,*

Of Mice and Men, *Tom's Midnight Garden,*

The Rivers of London, *Maze Runner,* *Holes,*

Ladybird's Peter and Jane, *The Runaway Train,*

Notes from a Small Island, *Schott's Miscellany,*

The Tale of Samuel Whiskers.

Not necessarily read (or loved) in that order.

Khan is unfaithful to cars. Lee has married and divorced so many cameras. Baz will swap and change between *KFC, Subway* and the local Fish 'n Chip shop '*Lord
of the Fries'* on a regular basis. Bell has of course been un-
true to a menagerie of women: big women, short women,
old women, young-ish, single, married, divorced. White

women with fake tans, black women with Jamaican nans and a 'new' woman with big hands. Women who rode motorbikes, women who drove escorts, women who were escorts plus a ladyboy on one occasion out in the east (not east as in Thailand but east as in Dagenham and Redbridge).

I find it difficult to change my tie on a daily basis. And don't ask me to change broadband provider. *Virgin* may sound more appealing, but I keep listening to *talktalk*.

It wasn't always the same. In university I swapped between my fab 4; a mesmerising line-up that didn't need Brian Epstein to manage them:

Lara, Mauritian, dark brunette hair, a face that melted my inner core, the most kissable, invitational lips and a pair of bum cheeks that were like two *space hoppers*.

Prity, Indian, the softest most beautiful skin and an intellect that attracted every mm of me.

Andi, from Kentucky (before we go any further, Andi is a she. 100% woman. I'm in touch with my feminine side – I can watch five minutes of *ITV*'s *'Loose Women'* and I once saw *'Call The Midwife'*. I'm totally hetro. Andi is a 'she'. American). The Statue of Beauty, the Grand Candy, Mount Lushmore, my perfect apple pie had she not moved back to the live in the USA in her Uncle Tom's cabin.

And Sylwia, a Polish exchange student that conveniently lost her passport whilst here; eyes that sparkled with life (and lust), blonde hair that danced on my skin and clenching muscles in her thighs that gripped like a dripping vice. I never did give her back her passport I'd hidden.

Remember the league ladders in the *'Shoot!'* magazines? These four were top of the table. Mauritius, India, USA and Poland – no wonder the lads called me 'Kofi Annan' – better to be nicknamed after the secretary general of the *UN* than Woody Allen.

But none of my fab 4 could put up with the fact that I had the 5th Beatle on my wall: a poster of Kelly Brooke. I should have taken it down.

Sophie didn't mind it. She ripped it off and binned it straight away. Sophie is 100% British. Born in Bodmin but they already had one beast so her family moved 'north' to Bristol. They soon moved from there for the same reasons a lot of people move out of Bristol.......because they live in Bristol! Her family then moved to either Clunton, Clunbury, Clungunford or Clun but finally 'emigrated' to Hay on Wye – an independent kingdom with a King of their own. So, in effect Sophie is foreign. Not quite Mauritius I know. But kind of 'foreign' all the same – pity you don't need a visa out of Hay on Wye.

But there is an idiom that says 'never tell a book by the cover' – Lara's front cover was truly sumptuous - most definitely 'beautifully bound'; she always looked enticing on my coffee table (and her back cover was pretty good too). You know, you're in *Waterstones* and you see '*A Clockwork Orange*' or '*When the Wind Blows*' or anything by Dr Seuss or '*Hand In Glove*' or '*Wuthering Heights*' and your eye is snared, allured towards a literary net; an illicit encounter with the illustration.....and you only went in to count how many Michael Morpurgo books they had.

Sophie's front cover? She was more *Fungus the Bogeyman* meets *the Gruffalo*. But and it's always a *big but* when it comes to Soph, I have to say I love those two covers AND I love what's inside those books. Time for a drink.

Baz shouted, "Pub stop."

We were making good time so Mr Thrush pulled up our wagon next to '*The Mollynogging*' public house, an ageing building ripe with cracking bricks and wrapped in a blanket of ascending ivy.

Twenty-two of us, a mob, pleased to be within the outskirts of Coventry. We'd show our Chinese visitors what a typical English country pub is like.

Empty.

Though it was scarce of people, it was full of spirit and fuller of spirits......and lagers......and even that diet cola for Alexa. She's not 18 till tomorrow.

"Welcome," came the booming voice of a diminu-tive pub landlady who couldn't have been more than four foot tall. She travelled behind her bar, manoeuvring on up-turned crates, jumping and side stepping from crate to crate. Her skin, cracking after years of sun scorched holidays in Torremolinos needs two million *Mills and Boon* books beneath it to make it more absorbent. This lady had character and a lot of decades behind her. She made Basil Thrush look like he'd not long been out of nappies. Actually, Basil is probably back in nappies at his age.

"Welcome to my pub one 'n all. Welcome to *The Mollynogging*. Oh yea." She spoke like a town crier and dressed like a Pearly Queen with beer mats sewn into her jacket.

This lady.....

"Call me Bapsie."

.....is getting shorter with each pint pulled. The antecedent of Augustus Gloop. The pub landlady.....

"Call me Bapsie   of *The Mollynogging.*"

....seemed to be shrinking as if in the land of the Houyhnhnms.

"Proud landlady of the best pub in the village."

The only pub in the village.

Above the bar, next to one of those *Big Mouth Billy Bass* mechanical fish was a sign which read, 'raise a glass to Tober-Na-Vuolich'. To the right of that was one of those dogs playing snooker pictures, then another, then another and another before a photo of the cast of *Auf Wiedersehen Pet.* Unsigned but nailed to the wall.

The Chinese friends enjoyed their 'real ales' so much that they ordered lagers.

We'd all been sprinting, knocked back two (or in Bell's case, three) drinks each, thanks to Khan's credit card, when Bell asked,

"Is it always this quiet in the *Mollynogging* Bapsie?"

"This is busy", she noted. "Busiest I've ever been."

"Yeah, yeah, I know   because of us lot   but if it wasn't for us, do you ever get busy?"

"Oh yes, Badger is in tonight. He popped off to the toilet just before you all came in."

"Should I check he's alright? That was about 20 minutes ago."

"No, give him another ten minutes and if he doesn't come out, we'll call in *Dyna-Rod Drain Services*   and the undertakers. He suffers."

"Ah   right   suffers with what?"

"Constipation luv. Too many pickled onions probably. But when he goes, he blows. It takes some flushing away, I tell ya. Needs more than a *shake n' vac.*"

Baz looked at his drink, looked at me. "Slap me in the face. Just want to check I'm not in some nightmare."

Bapsie added, "Just don't go in there after him. Last person that did ended up with mad cows."

Then he appeared. He must have been 6 foot 8, but with huge boots so perhaps 7 foot. A solid tree trunk of a dishevelled man; a greying, ripened beard and a decaying, haggard face pleated with creases. With an unquestionable fragrance. Hook, line and *stinker*.

As the door to the toilet flapped backwards and forwards, Badger's odour followed him. A cornucopian stench of a thousand burgers, each with a pickled onion and wrapped in the internal organs of roadkill.

"Busy tonight Baps."

"It is Badger. Same drink again? Coming up but I think you've had enough onions."

17

☑ University Reunion

☑ Road Trip (and painting experience!)

☒ Stag Party   ☑ Driving Test ~~Celebration~~

☑ 50th birthday   ☑ Thelma & Louise emptying

☑ New Job

☑ Just here for the beer (no onions)

☑ 18th birthday

☑ Big welcome to the UK ceremony x6

☒ Delivering goods to make money for his family

☑ Divorce Party

☑ Belated retirement party

☑ Jackpot win on the bingo x6   ☑ Bapsic and Badger

Back on the road. We didn't wave goodbye to

Big Onions Badger and the miniaturist Bapsie as they were coming with us. No room in the library so Bapsie locked up early and followed on her motorbike with Badger in the side car. *Wacky Races.*

We were going to make it. This night out I'd so looked forward to which, just a few hours before, looked like it was going to end stuck somewhere over *Mills and Boon* was on the cusp of being back on.

I'd managed to escape from Sophie's Alcatraz twice before. The latter was Mr Tickle's (his real name was Rick but he got the name Tickle because his arms were freak- ishly long) stag party trip to Amsterdam. I didn't even know Tickle Rick but Sophie was friends with his wife to be; and they all went away to a country retreat in the Cotswolds. We ended up retreating from Dutch countrymen. They took of- fence to Tickle's best man singing 'Tulips from Amster- dam' but changing the word 'tulips' to......'wankers'. Roger Hargreaves of *Mr Men* fame once asked, 'what does a tickle look like?' Well, he looked wet and scared shitless fleeing across a canal after being harangued by the locals. Seven of us and 30+ of them so we scattered like edam cheese rolling down Cooper's Hill. Dutch beer tastes strong. Dutch men look strong when angry. I found myself in the prostitute laden window-shopping district. 'When red light shows, stop here' we are told by *Highways England.* Not in the narrow alley I was in. It was keep walking, keep your head down and keep your head inside your pants. Windows were being tapped, bottoms slapped and hands beckoning men forward. It's amazing what 'drink me' potions, 'eat me' cakes and fuck me skimpy underwear can do to passers-by.

I later found out I was in the alley equivalent to Old Kent Road and Whitechapel. Some others had managed to find the red light equivalent to Park Lane, Mayfair and if you pass 'Go', collect 50 guilders as that's what it's going to cost to step through the looking glass and have 15 minutes being stunned by a stunner who gets tested weekly. The old bats in the lesser parts of the *monopoly* board I was lost in, were 25 guilders. Bargain. I refrained from a rash decision and a lifetime of....rashes.

The only other occasion I'd managed to wing an escape from the planet of the ape was a soaking umbrella-laden works bonding weekend in the north west. This involved a team-building treasure hunt, clay pigeon shooting, quad biking, a wealth of other 'experiences' and an afternoon in Blackpool – that was an experience in itself. The most memorable 'event' involved Debs Xerox (Debs from the accounts department got the nickname 'Debs Xerox' after a staff xmas party when she photocopied herself – she'd have got away with it but there was a paper jam and the boss panicked the next morning thinking it was a sales graph showing a double dip).

On the weekend away, she boosted staff morale by mounting a fine specimen of a horse. The horse bolted and Debs started to slip out of the saddle as she oscillated back and forth. She just managed to reach for the neck of the nag but her false fingernails slid against the reins in vain. In one last ditch attempt to regain composure (with the rest of her colleagues all watching with petrified pleasure, Debs engulfed her straggling legs around the barrel of her galloping steed. Ms Xerox gave out a horsey scream and appeared to be seconds away from a heavy fall. Joey (from the human resources department) could take no more and he saved her from being unseated by removing the plug. Debs skittishly got down from the motorised coin operated filly and we all left the pleasure beach for *the Hock n' Hoof* public house.

Back in the present day and just a mile down the back roads, Bapsie started flashing us. Headlights, not you know what. The last thing we wanted flashing was a little old lady not far off a telegram from the Queen with her pair of nibbles out.

Basil Thrush pulled over next to a row of shops. We were on the edge of the city. Civilisation. Pubs with people in. Bapsie galloped with her little legs from her contraption to our library. A Shetland pony jumping the edges of pavements.

Baz came to the window.

"Everything alright Baps?"

"It's Badger." We feared heart attack. Or severe constipation again. "It's onions." We feared a pickled sickness due to over-indulgence of the vegetable soaked in vinegar. "He fancies some more so he's going to go in the shop here to get some." We shouldn't have been relieved. We were.

"Fair enough," Baz uttered. "I'm going to grab some crisps." I joined him. We dodged the traffic and followed 'the onion badger' into the newsagents.

Badger was in and out (a bag of onions bagged up) quicker than most people spend on the toilet. Much quicker. Certainly much quicker than Badger takes on the toilet. He also had a copy of '*Blocked Pipes*', the monthly magazine for plumbers. Baz was scavenging the shelves, searching out any bargains as there's always a few unusual products on sale in one of these mini-market newsagents that no one else sells. Probably because those products often don't sell and that's why a mini-market always has them on sale.

The library was beeping the horn but purchasing crisps quickly was way off Baz's radar.

Another customer walked in. Looked like another bloke in a morphsuit. A black morphsuit. Another stag party? He went straight to the counter.

"Hand over all your takings," he said looking round. He hadn't noticed us. The in-store cameras had noticed him but his head was as covered as his feet. Baz was naked head and feet – everything in between clothed.

He grew impatient. "Money now. What's your name bitch?"

"Jules"

"Money now Jules."

Time to go back and get our Chinese Jackie Chan. But no time. The cashier was trembling. The hooded assailant had grabbed her neck and lumped a large bag on the counter next to several copies of *the Daily Star.* A rack of newspapers were also next to where I was hiding. The headline on the back page read, 'Shock Finances Put Football *Leagues Under the Sea*son Strain*'*.

The time 8.46 was signalled by a remarkable incident, a mysterious and inexplainable phenomenon which doubtless no one will ever forget.

I was frozen. Only the peas, fish fingers and *Vienetta* I'd retreated further towards were keeping me company. Baz was nowhere to be seen. Then I saw him in one of those round corner mirrors.

He was in the tinned section. He had a tin of baked beans in his hand. His throwing hand. I didn't see him launch it. I hardly saw it in the air; it was thrown with such force and it hit the man crack on the back of the head. Thud. Klonk. He fell forward.

Jules, a true shop assistant was 'happy to help' and broke his fall – the assailant's head landed in his own bag with his arms spread across the counter and only a *lotto* stand stopping his right leg from completely spreading out wider than it was engineered to do. If it was not for this *lotto* stand, his groin would have stretched beyond capability. *Thunderball.*

Baz calmly walked forward and checked he was completely knocked out (which he was). Baz then grabbed a handful of multipack bags of crisps of varying flavours and then queued up behind the assailant.

Jules, still in shock, moved to her spare till and asked Baz if he'd like to come across.

"Thanks," she said.

""I'll buy the baked beans tin too," Baz said.

"Actually, it's on me. My dad who owns the shop would kill me if I charged you for these crisps. You saved my life."

Baz and myself waited around. Her dad came down from upstairs. He'd been switching between old re-runs of *Open All Hours* and *Crimewatch UK.*

Law enforcement soon arrived. Apparently, the bloke was wanted as he'd done 56 newsagents in the past month. His 57th robbery was brought to a stop by Baz and a tin of *Heinz* baked beans. All captured on CCTV and already uploaded onto *youtube* by Jules' little brother Verne.

Jules' dad must have thanked Baz *20,000* times. A hero of our time. We were ready to go (the library had stopped beeping when the police turned up – they still had the remains of Thelma and Louise to keep them company).

We were just about to walk out of the shop when Badger walked back in.

"Any more onions out back?"

18

☑ University Reunion

☑ Road Trip (potential community award winner)

☒ Stag Party   ☑ Driving Test ~~Celebration~~

☑ 50th birthday   ☑ Thelma & Louise emptying

☑ New Job

☑ Just here for the beer (no onions)

☑ 18th birthday

☑ Big welcome to the UK ceremony x6

☒ Delivering goods to make money for his family

☑ Divorce Party

☑ Belated retirement party   ☑ Jackpot win on the bingo x6

☑ Bapsie and Badger record pub takings

Baz got a huge, feet stomping round of applause

back on the library. Not the first time he'd got the clap. The police had already been on board to explain to Mr Thrush and all, what had happened. Alexa had already found it on *Instagram* anyway, shared from *twitter*, re-posted to *facebook*, linked to snapchat, a slowed down clip looping on *TikTok* and there was a parody on *youtube* already. No mention on *Wikipedia* yet. The video had gone viral. 27,000 views before we were back on the road. *Come Dine With Me* must get fewer viewers on *Channel 4*. Over 1000 likes on fb and endless retweets before we'd hit the first set of traffic lights. '*Baz Baked Bean Hero*' as it was billed was all over the internet. But not one old fashioned dial-up to any of us about it. *Make someone happy with a phone call. British Telecom's Buzby* would be turning in his yellow feathery grave.

We were near the cathedral, circling a roundabout (several times as Basil Thrush was awaiting directions from Alexa but her phone signal was limited – probably, the Baked Bean Hero online frenzy was bringing the web down) when Baz burst out in tears. Proper tears. A toddler's tears. Water pouring from his eyes. You don't see that too often. I've never seen Baz cry. Even when that *swingball* hit him square in the testicles. I haven't seen an adult cry like this. Proper crying. Head in hands. Sudden. Lots of liquid splashing from the corner of his eyes. Not even Dylan Thomas cried that much when the police raided his university room and found him naked with a sheep. Dylan wasn't Welsh. His name wasn't even Dylan Thomas – he was called Mike Wood and he was from Greenwich - but we nicknamed him Dylan Thomas after the story broke. Dylan certainly had not gone gently into the good night. The police arrested him for indecency and 'Dylan' could not pull the wool over his thighs. No woman went 'under Mike Wood' again.

Baz was still crying. Ziv was first to unbuckle herself. Everyone moved one seat left or right. A *rubik's cube* of musical chairs so Ziv had space next to Baz. Mr Thrush likes everyone to be seat belted in.

"It's ok Baz. The shock of what you've done. It's just hit you sudden."

He tried to talk back but couldn't.

"Yeah Baz, " Bell beckoned back from the front of the library van. "It's the shock hitting you half hour later."

"No, nah, n ,no," Baz sniffled. "It's not that.   I don't think." You could hardly hear his words. "It's just, you know, my illness and all that. I just   just see like Baz, me, Baz   hero   and I thought, I mean, I like it   course but I won't be here to do it again. I'd swap it for another 20 years   another 2 years." His crying came back.

Ziv put her hand around Baz's shoulder just as we left another rotating roundabout (Alexa had given up on the sat nav and we were navigating via Bell's sense of smell for nightclubs).

We were stuck at another set of traffic lights. Baz, wiped his tears and looked up. "Fuck me," Baz said. "It's Animal."

We all looked to the right side of the library. About 20 yards ahead in the central reservation was 'Animal' – the outsider, a bloke we knew from university. We used to call him 'the graped crusader' from 'planet of the grapes' as legend has it, he only ate grapes. Then in the final year, he became 'Animal' – a mix of learning to play the drums and being crowned undisputed hedge jumping university champion (a little-known absurd sport where drunken students risk life and limb to jump hedges for no reason other than degrees in imbecility; yeah, universities.....where the great young minds in society gather for higher academic learning and research).

"I thought he was dead," Khan said.

"Yeah, he'd closed his *facebook* profile," Bell added.

I wanted to inform Bell that you can't shut your fb profile down if you're dead. By closing it, you must be alive.

The lights turned green. "Go slow Basil," Baz said.

Bell opened the window on the right behind the driver.

"Boom BOOM Animal, BOOM Boom An-i-mal," Bell screamed out.

"Can't believe you're still alive," Khan shouted. "I thought you were dead."

Animal heard a noise, turned and immediately....WHACK, our wing mirror smashed him.

"Fuck, we've just killed him," Khan said.

Basil pulled over. Me, Khan, Bell, Chinny and Baz all jumped out, yomping towards the unfortunate scene. We all knew him when he was alive. WL came too.

"I can do mouth to mouth," she said.

"She'll bloody crush him," Chinny whispered across to me.

We held back. He wasn't moving. A dead carcass. Lifeless. The wing mirror was shattered too.

"Chinny, you knew him best at uni. Go over and check for a pulse," I suggested. "The rest of us will stay back just in case."

Chinny laboured over, hesitating. Not a pleasant sight to see anyone dead, especially when we've killed him.

Chinny leaned over Animal. His eyes were shut. Chinny looked back and signalled bad news by shaking his head. They were beneath a streetlamp. *A certain slant of light* was beaming down on Animal's body. Crepuscular rays spreading to form Animal's ladder to the skies. He knelt down next to Animal.

Someone was looking at him – *a* disturbing feeling when *you're dead.*

Animal opened one eye. It shut. Probably an involuntary after death twitch. The other eye opened. It shut. A corpse still breathing. Just. Both eyes opened.

"Am I in heaven?" Animal muttered.

Chinny said nothing in return.

Animal summoned the will to speak again: "Am I in God's heaven?"

"No," Chinny said puzzled. "No, you are on earth." Chinny turned and mouthed over, "delirious, concussed probably   bang on head but alive."

Animal suddenly shot up and grabbed Chinny by the throat.

"Why you dressed as Jesus then?"

We all rushed over (except WL who had obviously been waiting for the chance to save his life, become a hero and have a *youtube* video named 'Attractive lady saves wing mirror slain man with kiss of life').

"Animal, Animal, relax. It's Chinny. Let go of Jesus," we shouted.

We carried him back to our little red wagon. He took the final seat. We were full. Bapsie and Badger still following in their chariot.

We were in Coventry. Now, we've just got to find the place.

"Any ideas?" I asked in one job lot.

"Follow the North Star," Chinny shouted back, buckling himself to the seat next to that squirrel which was by the side of the donkey. We've got enough wise men.

19

☑ University Reunion

☑ Road Trip (potential community award winner)

☒ Stag Party   ☑ Driving Test ~~Celebration~~

☑ 50ᵗʰ birthday   ☑ Thelma & Louise emptying

☑ New Job

☑ Just here for the beer (no onions)

☑ 18ᵗʰ birthday

☑ Big welcome to the UK ceremony x6

☒ Delivering goods to make money for his family

☑ Divorce Party

☑ Belated retirement party   ☑ Jackpot win on the bingo x6

☑ Bapsie and Badger   ☑ Animal finding religion

Everything had gone wrong today. Everything had gone right. We'd travelled between *cities* but it was *the tale of two* separate days within less than 24 hours.

It was the best of times, it was the worst of times. It was the age of absolute senseless stupid foolishness.

We were here but we couldn't collect our '*triangular cycling proficiency badge*' because we couldn't find the sodding nightclub. Bell, for once, came up with a cunning plan – he normally comes up with cunnilingus.

"We're going to an over 35's nightclub yeah? Well, just follow over 35's looking people. They'll lead us into temptations."

So, we did. Not easy in seminal darkness. Bit dodgy trawling older looking people in a mobile library at walking pace. A motor vehicle at 2mph followed by a wheezing motorbike sidecar at 2mph followed by a chain of irate vehicles behind at 2mph. Old age and road rage.

On the road, the slow-moving vehicle was compli-
mented by a string of fast-moving conversations. The chat-
ter throughout the library was punctuated by horns and
beeps from passing vehicles. Only one of the abusive cars
had a 'little person on board' sign though there was no actual person in that car bar the fist waving driver. Off the wall
peculiarities that become 'on the windscreen' normalisa-
tion.

First up Tonka and Lee:

"I like your T-shirt. Is that a spaceship?"

"No, it's a *Delorean* car   from *Back to the
Future.*"

"So, is that like a make of shirt? Like *Nike, Vans,
Adidas.....*"

"No, A *delorean* or *DMC Delorean* to give it an official name was the only car manufactured by *DMC* in the
early 1980's. Designed by Giorgetto Giugiaro, the sports car
had gull-wing doors. It went from zero to sixty in 8.8

seconds with a manual transmission. Only nine thousand *Deloreans* were actually made before production ceased."

"Thanks," Tonka found a gap in Lee's breathing to interrupt.

"I could go on if you'd lik----"

"No, No, You've explained it well."

Though Lee appears abnormal to be wearing a vintage shirt, maybe he's the normal one. Most people wear brands on the outside of their shirts these days. We're walking adverts.

I dropped in on Dumper and Baz's conversation:

"You could advertise baked beans now Baz. Or better still, you could help food banks by encouraging the people to take tins to food banks."

"Nah, bollox to that. Most people I know who use food banks don't need it. They've got fifty-inch tellies, a life supply of roll ups, a food cupboard full of alcohol, four dogs that eat money and a phone that's not exactly an old *nokia*. Cut out the fags, sell the TV, cut down on the booze, just have one dog, drop the phone contract and buy yourself some proper food. And you can play '*snake*' on the *nokia*."

"Yeah, but the food bank really helps some people."

"Yeah, some people yeah. Others take the piss. It's a BANK. Deposit your fifty-inch tv in there and then the interest on it is your food. Deal. Give. Stop taking."

Over to Animal and Chinny:

"Jesus   ha   ha.   I mean god, that scared me. I thought I'd died."

" God's offering a first class service then for you. No grim reaper. Send Jesus down to bring Animal back to heaven."

"Good to see you again Chinny."

"Man, it's been ages. We were the double expresso. Morecambe and Wise. Terry and June. Chinny and Animal."

"You know, us being always together, people thought we were homosexual," Animal said.

"Really? Nothing wrong if we had been but can't help you there Animal. Closest I come to it is being 'homersexual' – I quite fancy Marge Simpson."

"Ha, well, I'm pansexual – really get horny when I'm washing up frying pans....."

I cut out and turned to Bell and Khan talking football.

"Who do you support Khan?"

"I don't support anyone because I don't like football."

"I support West Ham United for the very same reasons."

"Oh, West Ham Bell? Is that the 'I'm forever blowing bubbles' team?

"You can't say that now Michael Jackson's dead. Offensive to his monkey. He took that monkey everywhere. Australia, Japan, South Africa, Norway, Finland, Iceland. Did you know blow jobs are banned in Iceland?"

"Really Bell? Why Iceland? Why there and not like Denmark or Sweden?"

"They just are in *Iceland*. And they're banned in *Sainsbury's* and *Tesco's*."

Khan enjoyed Bell's unrefined approach to humour but was ready to move on and change direction.

"Let's give up," Khan said to everyone. "Let's fill Thelma and Louise in an off-license, pull off the main street, into a layby and have our own party."

The idea was tempting and everyone would have given it some thought but the police were back. A flashing blue light. No chance of it being Uncle Rog. The Chinese took cover. Their time in the UK was no doubt up. They'd gone through enough with us. The home office should put Baz at all harbours, airports and in the middle of the English Channel – his idea of a road trip canvassed to all incoming refugees will make them head back to France. It's France after all. Why try to cross the channel in rubber dinghies risking precious lives when you're already in France? Baguettes, the patisseries and boulangeries which are *tasty tasty very very tasty*, the Iron Lady (not Maggie Thatcher but the Eifel Tower), Riviera beaches, traffic free motorways, golden open countryside, chateaus, wine, camembert, brie, onions (yes, onions – tell Badger), champagne and *Joe Le Taxi*. As refugees are fleeing the safety of France, we're all hopping across there on our holidays.

The siren stopped. Three police cars and a police van. They're taking us all away. Two additional unmarked cars trapped us from the front and a further van pulled up alongside us. An assemblage of police officers got out, swarming towards us. They lined up and saluted as a senior officer stepped out from a police car with one of those mini flags on it. She must have been the Chief Constable. Letters after her name. More important than *Cagney AND Lacey.* They all approached our library.

A police officer stepped on board followed by the chief.

"Good evening officer," Chinny said. An unusual sight, Jesus shaking hands with a police officer.

"Good evening," said the officer, nodding towards the rest of us and glancing again at the Chinese group. "I'll pass you on to our Chief Superintendent who needs to say a few words." There was a domino effect of gulps scattering among us all.

"Where's Baz?" she said.

Baz made himself known by standing up.

"I'd like to thank you.   You've made a difference to the greater good. I won't go into details. There will be a press conference tomorrow but what I will say is the man you,   you   baked beaned...." There were several chuckles including her own officers. "......yes, the man you baked beaned if I can call it that, was a very dangerous criminal and you've   um   done the country a service. No doubt some kind of reward stroke   commendation. But for now,   my team of officers, would like to take a few photos with you."

The police waiting in the cold outside gave three cheers for Baz as ma'am vacated the library with Baz. Numerous photos with groups and with individuals wanting Baz selfies. Baz got back on the bus. The police back in their van and cars. Very nice and well deserved but slowed us down even more.

"Good news," Baz declared. "We're getting an eight vehicle police escort all the way to the club."

20

☑ One mobile library filled

☑ A motorbike and sidecar

☑ Multi-vehicle police escort

We were there in no time. Journey to the end of the night. We should have hit a criminal from our own town (there's enough of them) with a tin of spaghetti hoops at 8am and got a police escort all the way. But we are here now. The over 35's nightclub. Almost 15 years too late as most of us are nearing 50. But we're here before Basil Thrush hits 100 (his age; Basil didn't get above 48pmh driving the library).

We were wanting to get off the library before Basil put it in neutral and before Badger gets himself locked in the toilet area but Lee hesitated.

"Looking forward to this......I think," Lee smiled a little. "I haven't been to a disco for years."

"I was in a club last month," Bell said. "DJ played *'You Spin Me Round (like a record)'* so I just did loads of spins. Next he played *'Jump'* so I jumped up and down. Then he played *'Come On Elieen'* and that's when they kicked me out. Eileen hasn't phoned me since. To be honest, I don't miss her. She always tried too hard to be all sexy like. Sliding her lollypop in and out of her *'you know what'* and then licking it. I told her 'don't do that as you'll need it Monday morning to help the kids across the road'. But she didn't listen. I only stayed with her coz she made the absolute best red lentil curry with rice. Actually, do you know what's the difference between a chickpea and a lentil?"

Lee replied with a bewildered 'no' – the rest of us just wanted to get off the vehicle (and / or away from Bell).

Bell jumped off the library and bellowed back with, "I've never had a lentil on my face."

Wiping that comment from our memory, we stared in admiration at our new home. Even from the carpark, the club looked awesome. Entertainment oozed from the darkened establishment. Peeling promotional posters dispersed within the undeniable crumbling paintwork. State of the art sound proofing. An atmosphere inside that must be kept inside. No lights escaping from the place. No queueing at the door either. We were elevated, ready to hoof it on the dancefloor to 'who lets the dogs out', all set for a flock of mutton dressed as lamb. Dylan Thomas not invited.

Baz was off the library first. A road trip to remember. Our hero. Our tour-guide. Our organiser. Our *Captain Corelli*.

Dr Baz had enjoyed a day in which no one had died (not even Animal).

"It's closed," Baz revealed, no longer excited or full of beans.

"What, full up?"

"No closed. Closed down. Shut last month."

The sign on the door was clearer:

The management *would like to THANK ALL our loyal*
customers over the past 27 years in ~~buzness~~ business. You
are our friends and our clients.

You have been with us for all these good years and we
thank you for your custom. We regret that we are seasing
buisness from imedyate afect

The management   May 12th

Bell added further clarity:

"What the fuck?"

Khan translated, "They've been open 27 years and
the one day we decide to come, they're shut......

FuckBolloxShit."

21

For only the second time, I was pleased to see a text message from Sophie. I needed the distraction. The only other occasion I welcomed her unreadable characters was when she texted to say 'too much snow had fallen during *Trish's Tuppy Party'* - party? Sales pitch with Tupperware more like. Sophie said she'd bought some Tupperware. A few plastic containers off Trish, the party plan host but I definitely saw batteries on the handwritten receipt.

The unexpected snow meant they all had to bed down at Trish's and she wouldn't be back till next morning. It was beautiful. And it got better and better. More snow fell and they were all there for three nights. Trish's husband

243

hired a digger in the end to get rid of them all. Bloody climate change. Not happened since.

SOS: < Baz is all over media. Famous emoji trophy > 10.45pm

SOS: < Y did you not throw the baked bean tin emoji bicep > 10.47pm

SOS: < U could been famous LOL emoji 2x trophy > 10.48pm

< Yeah, I know. He did great > 10.50pm

SOS: < so, ur fone battery miracle re-charge happened emoji skull and crossbones > 10.51pm

Plank. I walked into that. She's always one step ahead and two biscuits ahead too. I started typing an excuse.

SOS: < Do not type an excuse emoji thumbs down > 10.52pm

SOS: < anyway, hope u r havin a good time emoji thumbs up > 10.53pm

SOS: < I going 2 bed emoji cucumber > 10.53pm

SOS: < Just thought I tell u that Baz fame & was on TV emoji TV > 10.54pm

< TV? Internet you mean > 10.55pm

SOS: < Yeah internet fb, *youtube* insta the lot but TV too. *Sky news ITV BBC* emoji globe > 10.57pm

SOS: < u know the last item feel good slot on news emoji laughing face > 10.57pm

< Wow. Thanks saggy. I'll tell him > 10.58pm

SOS: < Ok go back to dance floor and enjoy yourself emoji kissing face > 10.58pm

< Thanks x > 10.59pm

Ten texts to say Baz is on the television. And people say communication is dying. It's dead. Nailed to a cross and cremated, hung, drawn and quartered, flayed, burned at the stake and stretched on the rack..............but still watching *Love Island.*

There was a tap on my shoulder. I turned to see two gold teeth inside a cave of a mouth. They belonged to a man I immediately nicknamed (in my head) 'Gold'. His sheepskin coat was a tanned colour. Five rings (golden), rock hammers for fists, a chain (golden) dangling from his neck, glasses trimmed in gold and just a few strands of hair looping over his balding head (the hair was silver). He tightened his own tie. "You Baz?"

"No." My words jumped straight back. I am not anyone people like him ask for. Two troglodytic larger men stepped out of the shadows from behind him. These two were a sub-species, knuckle-walking towards us.

"Where is he?" the broader, slighter shorter silver-backed one asked.

Baz stepped out of the shadows. More of a bare foot *Morris dance* than a menacing thud.

"I'm Baz. Who wants me?"

"Ehhhhh," all three smiled, cracking their knuckles like animalistic gangsters. Gold lifted his hammer hands up and pinched Baz's cheek with his first finger and thumb.

"My boy."

Shit, is this Baz's dad I thought?

"Baz........you've done the country proud. Baked beans. Genius."

The content was endearing. The tone still gruff.

"Do you know who I am Baz?" Gold said beating his own chest.

"No."

"I'm not only Mayor of a nearby town but I own this club you're standing outside."

"Oh, nice," Baz said looking at the urine stained walls of the club.

"I hear you want to go in. Don't answer that. You're going in. I'm opening it up for one more night in honour of you."

"Wow. Thanks Mr Mr Mayor."

"BUT," Gold bellowed, grabbing Baz by the shirt and prodding his face forward, "Don't go throwing any baked bean tins about as the demolition are in next week to knock it all down so I can build flats on it."

Baz joined in laughing nervously with the two henchmen who'd stepped back into the shadows again. Gold looked at me. I laughed.

"Right, open it up and you two work the door. Free entry to anyone who knows Baz."

We thanked Gold who shouted over a female called Curvar. She was originally from Portugal; his cleaner cum speciality fish chef cum personal assistant PA cum wife-to-be cum person he's putting in charge to dish out the free alcohol to us. Gold then disappeared around the front with his henchmen. They'd been introduced as Browne and Anthony – their mandibles protruded further than their maxillas; gorillas in shirts with muscles popping out everywhere. Now, we were all on the 'people you might know' recommended friends list on *facebook*.

Curvar smiled. She looked at Baz.

"You want soapy hand job?"

Baz smiled back. Then it registered.

"Say that again?"

"You want soapy hand job? She smiled again, miming her hands rubbing together. Friendly couple Gold and Curvar. "If you want soapy hand job, I help you. She unzipped her *Gucci* (imitation, but she didn't know that) handbag. Gift from Gold. Probably part of the pre-nup. She reached in with her delicate hand; nodding enthusiastically at Baz; and she pulled out a small bottle of hand gel. "Here. Bottle of hand job. You use please. Use on hands yeah. As very painty yeah. This soapy hand job will help you."

"Ahh, soapy hand gel. Thanks Curvar."

I look forward to the day when Curvar tells all Gold's fellow dignitaries at the council meetings that, 'I give you fish and you men ate them' as I'm sure it will sound like, 'I give you fist-ing hu-mil-i-ation'. Either way, they get filled up.

Baz, missing out on the soapy hand job, was just pleased to be getting 4.7% free alcohol in the lagers Curvar would be passing on and 60% free alcohol in the hand-gel.

"Phew," I said. "Result. Gold's like the bloke in *American Psycho* out of the cuckoo's nest with a bit of *Pudsey Bear* thrown in."

"I don't care. We're going in," Baz said marching off to tell the others.

'Abandon all hope' is printed *in blood red lipstick on the walls of the* club.

Baz had already spread the news and formed a line at the door as Gold and his henchmen opened up from the inside.

One of the henchmen (Anthony or Browne, I get the gorillas mixed up. Let's call him henchman one) boomed his voice down the queue: "Free bar thanks to Mr Flinch here," pointing at Gold (aka The Mayor), "in honour of Baz. No DJ though. Anyone know how to?"

"I'll do it," said Berol. Basil Thrush put his head in his hands. This was no time for 'DJ BJ'.

Khan piped up, "Alexa will do it via her phone." She nodded. Henchman one pointed at Alexa. Mr Thrush looked relieved. We wouldn't be listening to Buddy Holly songs. That'll be the day I thought.

"Right, in you come," signalled henchman two.

We were excitedly bundling in. The henchmen (one and two) looked amazed at the unique range of clientele: From Jesus to new Disc Jockey Alexa, from Bapsie to Badger, Bell to WL, Mr Thrush footslogging in the doors to Lee asking the henchmen to smile for the camera.

Baz and myself were last to go in.

"Sorry Baz. You can't come in," henchman two said. He pointed at a torn club rules sign sellotaped to the door: 'Point six – footwear that meets club standards.'

"Rules are rules," Gold said smirking.

"You serious Mr Flinch?"

Gold yanked his neck in the direction of a room that said 'STORE'. "Get Anna Conda's shoes." He turned to us. "He left them in there after a gig two months ago. They'll fit."

The henchmen returned bringing back a perfect set of size ten shoes. Red, glittery, sparkling shoes with seven-inch heels that Mick the scaffolder uses when performing as Anna Conda.

Baz *dragged* his feet into them and we were in.

22

☑ Destination OPEN....and for one nite only, Baz in Anna Conda's shoes

DJ Alexa was ripping up the tunes and the dance-floor was like newly boxed popcorn: packed, bouncing and spilling over. In reality, it was just Tonka, Dumper, WL, Dusty, BJ and Skinny Latte on the sticky parquet flooring but it was packed – those six townspeople of *Brobdingnag* would fill Dartmoor, The Lake District or any open space........even between Bell's ears.

The free bar was gashing open. A waterfall of gratuitous booze flowing. Khan and Baz surfing the intoxicating waves.

Bell was nowhere to be seen. I walked into the toilets. Two cubicles were taken. Obviously, Badger was trying to offload onions in one. The strains were audible over the boom boom of Kylie's '*I can't get you outta my head*'. I wanted to change 'head' to 'arse' but I just hummed it instead. Bell exited from the other cubicle. His face flushed, mottled, ashen.

"You alright Bell? You don't look well."

His eyes were sunken. Pained blotches on his face. Bell walked in an uneasy manner, looking like he'd been hammering a radish into his bottom with a mallet.

"Haemorrhoids mate."

His bum seemed to hover above his legs, isolated from the rest of his body. He clunked forward, exhausted and irritated by the accuracy of the homing air-to-surface missile of affliction. A weapon of mass discomfort.

"Go to the Natural History Museum and look at the model of a baboon's arse. That's how I feel. I should apply for disability living allowance. Any negative effect that you've had for 12 months or more and you're disabled under the DDA."

I'm sure the government officials coming to check on Bell's criteria for disability would be expecting epilepsy or bipolar or cerebral palsy. There's no tick box on their form for haemorrhoids. Piles of paperwork.

"It's easing," Bell said, wanting to itch himself one more time but knowing one soothing itch would result in a *domino rally* of the medical term '*Prolonged VIP': vexation in posterior.* Or as I prefer to say, once the jacksie taxi starts, the journey to *Anusol* is just a few itches away.

Bell knew the more he talked, the less likely he'd be to rub against his rawness: "I think there should be a march. Like Gay Pride. An annual event   ROIDS PRIDE. We're a minority group."

"A march would be good. But no events that involve sitting down," I chipped in.

"It's because I eat too much. Not enough fruit and veg. Doctor said it's down to my high carbs diet."

"No soya, that's what it is."

"Soya?"

"Yeah, SOYA – sitting on your arse."

We walked to the main doors. A *dog* was *barking in the night-time. A curious incident* but we ignored it.

It was minutes after midnight. The dog was in the middle of the pavement in front of Mr Flinch's (Gold aka The Mayor) club.

Traffic was approaching.

The dog leapt up and ran towards some bins. Two exhausted buses pulled up outside the club. Both coaches were laden with ladies. I did not see one male within the rumbustious sect except for the driver of 'bus 2'. The females all looked to be in their 30's, 40's, 50's – if they're coming into the club, they're going to bring the average age down a bit.

They seemed in the mood to party. Bell caught the eye of a strawberry haired lady about seven seats back. She had a mullet perm that was so 1970's high, it could have been used to sail the *Black Pearl* across the Caribbean. She's probably a respectable head teacher, vicar, accountant or county court magistrate. She slammed her body against the window and lifted up her top. No bra, just a pair of wobbly melons. On one breast, it said, 'Jason' scribed in big orange marker pen. The other breast was marked with the name 'Howard'.

"I'd like to see where Gary, Mark and Robbie are," Bell said. "You've got to remember two things: Number one, I'm like a female ferret. If I don't have sex for a year, I will die. Number two, I am a breast man."

"You're a big tit more like."

"*Fantastic breasts and where to find them* – that will be the next book I write."

Driver of 'bus 1' stepped down from her bus. She had *scrunchies* on her wrists but they were redundant in their role as her hair was tight to her head. Bell almost needed a hairdresser more than she did. The driver probably knows Heather the tattooist as her arms were blazoned with skulls, crossbows, barbed wire, eagles, a sniper gun plus one and only one celebrity name – Chesney Hawkes – his name inside a heart inside a butterfly inside a hand grenade.

"Club open?"

"No but yes," I said hoping the shapeless of face skinhead bus driver was asking for her nymphomaniac passengers and not just her maniac self. "I can ask Gold um   Mr Flinch if you can come in his club   if that's what you want," I added.

Bell disagreed, "Bollox to that. Mr Flinch said any of Baz's friends can come in. Baz will try to befriend you all when you come in. Sorted."

The bus driver put her thumbs up to 'bus 2'.

"Thanks," she said. "We've been to the exhibition venue for the '*Bake That*' show." We looked puzzled. "They're a tribute act that sing *Take That* songs whilst the audience bake and eat cakes."

Bell's eyes were glazed.

Baking cakes, eating cake and *Take That* music. *Bake That?* Genius money making. I should have thought of that. Sophie will be at the show next year no doubt. Let's hope they hold it in the Winter and it snows.

The *Bake Thatters* boogied their way into the club. The feisty first few all stopped to say hello and fizgigged their names to us as they passed: Rebecca, Nadja, Camilla, Carrie, Justine, Emma, Kim all looking delicious and nutritious. Then a hideous kinky one with green eyes who introduced herself as Frankie. Bell whispered, 'Frankenstein more like'. The henchmen heaved the second door open and the rest of the *Bake Thatters* all flooded through in one surge. The swarm of excitement – for all of us.

The strawberry haired (proud of her melons) head teacher (probably) who was towards the back of the line, stopped herself by Bell.

"I am bursting for the ladies," she quipped.

Bell was bursting for a lady too. Anyone would do but she'd just jumped in his trolley. He was a blind man with a pistol. Loaded.

"Need the loo luv. Gagging. But I want to catch up with you inside." She kissed him on the cheek and winked.

"Catch you inside," Bell said, his haemorrhoids gone (for the time being). "Look forward to that," he said nudging me.

'It only takes a minute', I thought.

Returning to the club interior, the dancefloor was now over spilling to all areas of the room. Alexa had caught whiff of the needs of the bus passengers (their Take That t-shirts were probably good enough clues) and she'd succumbed to demand by supplying '*Could It Be Magic*' followed by '*Relight My Fire*'.

Frankie, the girl with the green eyes kept looking over towards me. Her playful attention encouraged me to allow myself to be summoned. She was more queen of the beasts than kittenish; all the same, teasing and appreciation can do a lot for a shopper, particularly a consumer like me who's not eaten (or been fed by Sophie) for years; especially when it's a bargain like Frankie. I prayed: 'Please God, keep me faithful.....but not just right now'.

Frankie was like one of those special buys in the middle aisles of *Aldi* or *Lidl*. You don't need an inflatable kayak, a new screwdriver set, dot-to-dot books, one size fits all gym gear or any more bird feeders but when there, it's an impulse buy and it goes in your trolley. Frankie is that aerated kayak and right now, I'm inflating and off to the checkouts. The *RNLI* advise strongly against inflatable use. Frankie certainly has big waves and there's no lifeguard on duty on this beach. I deflate myself. I'll go home and return to Sophie's dry dock.

Alexa was now playing '*Pump Up The Volume*' - I don't need reminding of anything being pumped up so I request the song, '*Born to Hand Jive*' and it's true. Bell is the quickest hand jobber ever seen. He owned the dancefloor.

Alexa kept the place buzzing with '*Greased Lightning*' followed by:

Heaven 17's '*Temptation*' – nymphet Frankie keeps sending flirtatious smiles over.

Shania Twain's '*Man I Feel like a Woman*' – what Bell has nightmares about after his ladyboy 'moment' in Dagenham and Redbridge.

The Bangles' '*Walk Like an Egyptian*' – what Bell went through the next day.

Sister Sledge's '*Frankie*' – not that I needed prompting.

Ashford and Simpson's '*Solid*' – an aide-memoire relating to Badger's deposit in the toilets.

Alexa batted between 70's, 80's and 90's music just to keep everyone happy:

Karma Chameleon   Ebenezer Goode

Yes sir I can Boogie   D.I.S.C.O.   99 Red Balloons

Tainted Love   Baker Street   Spirit In The Sky

Don't Leave Me This Way

I think We're Alone now   Theme from S'Express

Ride on Time   Two Tribes   Insanity   Scatman

.....and......   *Ooh Aah Just a Little Bit*

Throwing in a bit of Arnold Van Buren just to keep herself sane whilst declining Bapsie's choice of 1950's *'Rock around The Clock'*. She did relent to *'Great Balls Of Fire'* from the same decade but only as a 'shout out' to Chinny, who was suffering from groin rash due to being in that lycra morphsuit too long earlier. Time for him to change (*as if by magic*) into his third fancy dress outfit – the firefighter.

Alexa did put on a one-minute blast of *'Kung Fu Fighting'* just to get the Chinese six up. It didn't work but they went crazy when she accidentally swiped Rick Astley's *'Never Gonna Give You Up'*.

Firefighter Chinny appeared to be having a fit during *'The Rhythm of the Night'*. You can't call his movements dancing. His arms were listening to a different beat to the rest of his flailing body. His elbows were heli-copters without supervision. He didn't require paramedics. Unlike the Thrush's. Mrs Thrush 'sprinted' (a slow walk that needed a *zimmer frame*) towards 'hubby' and tried to emulate the Dirty Dancing 'lift'. '*Time of My Life*' it cer-tainly wasn't. *Flat Stanley*. The paramedics had to remove Basil's ankle, wedged between Berol's bum cheeks. This never happened to Torvil and Dean doing *the Bolero*. Alexa distracted the squeamish melee of onlookers with Queen's '*Fat Bottomed Girls*' and all turned out well. The paramedics stayed as their shift was now over.

The police returned. Their shift was still going on but they'd had enough of violent drug crime and decided our venue was more suited to community policing. Little did they know that Chinny had a police record and I don't mean '*Every Breath You Take*' or '*Don't Stand So Close To Me*'. He was driving back to university 28, maybe 29 years ago. Speeding. A cop pulled him over, leaned into his window and said, 'Papers....'. Chinny shouted, 'Scissors. I win.' And drove off. The car was registered to his parents.

They got a letter through the post. No message in a bottle. Big fine. Court appearance. His parents were crushed. So was the car.

Alexa got down from the stage. She pressed continue on a playlist called '*slow moving songs*'. The contents of the dancefloor gave her a rousing cheer followed by applause and stomping feet. She walked over to Mr Thrush, he gave her something and she left for the exit, stopping to talk to one of the henchmen on her way. Her playlist started automatically.

The first song:

'*My Heart Will Go On*' by Celine Dion.

I've never been so relieved to hear it. I checked my phone just in case. Elation. It wasn't Sophie. I started slow dancing by myself. Someone with green eyes was looking over to me. Forbidden fruit. She put her drink down and started wandering over. Every little thing she does is magic.

I didn't know what to do to be frank.

23

 Frankie.....yes or no?

A man swept past Frankie, pinballing her off in another direction. He moved through the mist of swaying couples as James Blunt's 'You're Beautiful' started up. He received a leg up off Chinny (should have been a fireman's lift). Up onto the stage and pressed 'stop' on the playlist. A crescendo of booing rang out around the room. The head teacher dancing in Bell's arms looked relieved. She wiped his dribble from her chin. The lights came on. I had throwback visions of Sophie reading aloud. The booing ceased fire. It was Gold looking menacing. He wasn't menacing. He was just looking it. It's what he does. It's how he got to be Mayor.

"Bad news folks. It's 2am. That's it. Time to shut up or I'll lose my license."

A clear shout echoed from the side of the stage. "It's ok. Another hour is ok."

Gold turned at leisure, squinting in the light. Now he was menacing. Someone had dared question his guidance. "Who said that?" Gold bellowed.

"Over here." A hand went up. "It's me. Chief of Police."

"Oh, that's alright then. Let's get the party restarted." He swiped Alexa's phone. A roulette wheel of songs rolled round. "Do you feel lucky punks?" Gold shouted as he stepped down from the stage. I don't think Gold made his money from the football pools coupons as luck wasn't his middle name – the song '*Agadoo*' randomly started up. Definitely not a score draw.

Gold pulled me towards him (*to the left, to the right, jump up and down and to the knees*) as he passed and rammed some words down my ear that sounded like 'I ain't even got a license anymore but good to keep in with the police, eh'.

'*Agadoo*' moved into '*YMCA*' which moved back to Black Lace with '*Superman*'. '*It's Raining Men*', *Dancing Queen*', '*Staying Alive*', *So Macho*' and that little-known party song, '*Gangnam Style*'.

I was looking over at Chinny who was trying to teach Bapsie the moves of 'Gangnam Style' when two hands wrapped me from behind, covering my eyes. I could just about fathom out the words 'Guess Who?' Not a party game I really wanted to play at 2.20am.

"Give up." *My struggle* was evident as I aided the unblinding of my eyes, turned and couldn't believe it. The bloody Nazi. Steve Stevenson. He was given the very poor taste nickname of Nazi because of his SS initials. The bloke was as un-Nazi like as anyone. He'd make Gandhi look like a fascist. Steve likes painting and fine arts, he has a passion for architecture and music plus Steve's a non-smoker and vegetarian. Actually, exactly the same as Hitler. Only difference is Steve was never nominated for a *Nobel Peace Prize*.

Steve wasn't keen on his Nazi nickname but he put up with it though our insistence on calling every girl he dated 'Eva Braun', to her face, didn't help with long lasting relationships for him.

Today fate chose Steve to be here.

To Steve's left stood Gwyneth Paltrow. Not the real one. But one of those celebrity look-a-likes.

It was poor visibility (Chinny had ignited the smoke machine – bloody firefighters) but even I knew it wasn't the real Ms Paltrow. At least, I hoped it wasn't. The last thing I want gorgeous Gwyneth seeing me in is a '*Chopper*' t-shirt. I'd changed out of '*Drooper*', one of the *Banana Splits* after Khan used it to wipe blood off his face. He was bloodied as he'd failed to open a bottle of beer with his teeth. His party-piece. Not anymore. Learn hand-jiving Khan.

I'd had experiences with look-a-likes before. I once booked a Britney Spears look-a-like but her apparition was more like Judy Finnigan. I also went to a party and berated a really unsimilar Bob Carolgees and Spit the Dog look-a-like but was later told they were the real ones.

"Let me introduce my wife-to-be.   This is Kate."

Phew. It's not the real Gwyneth Paltrow. I can keep my *Chopper* t-shirt on. But hang on, Gwyneth's middle name is Kate (how do I know that? I don't obsess about her. Honest) – maybe calling her Kate is a ruse to hide her real identity. I should test her cover by shuffling Alexa's playlist to find '*Paradise*' by Cold Play – that would wind her up and send her running for the sliding doors.

Chinny, Baz, Khan and Lee all shipped in. Bell dislodged his head from the cleavage of the headmistress and joined us.

"Steve, you made it."

"What you doing here Steve?"

"SS Nazi boy   about time."

"You missed the bus journey. Actually, we all did"

"I took your place Steve, been filming it all."

...were the various responses to the Steve Stevenson surprise visit.

"I pulled out of my own stag party. Bad form I know. Sorry again Baz. But Kate here had double booked me on a romantic weekend in Stratford-Upon-Avon. We stopped off at Sarehole Mill on the way. You guys know I love '*Lord of the Rings*'. So, as you can imagine, with getting married and all that, I couldn't really disappoint, especially as it was five-star hotel."

Khan seemed to nod once he heard the hotel had five stars.

"But then Kate started laughing as I was taking off my slippers for bed. She'd been scanning social media. She said some bloke had hit a big crim on the bonce with a baked bean tin. I couldn't believe my eyes. I said I know that bloke. And Kate said let's go find him."

"How did you know we were here?"

"I phoned Sophie. Not happy. Woke her up."

"She's not happy asleep or awake," I added.

"But she told me where you all were. We came, we saw and you conked him on the head   with baked beans. I mean,   man,   legend you are."

I couldn't believe we were all back together. The six of us. Plus Lee. The cameraman is a legend himself. And he loaned me his retro t-shirts (I have to give them both back after washing them in non-bio powder at less than 50 degrees. Strict instructions). So, seven of us. Seven brothers. Midnight's Children. Seven of Us. Magnificent. Well, either magnificent or deadly sins. Bell would be gluttony. He was soon back in the bosom slow dancing to Shania Twain's 'You're Still the One'. Still the one? He definitely had his face between two.

We were all in *a room of one's own.*

But, we asked you about women, baked beans and fiction.

I pulled Steve over to one side.

"Have you heard about Baz and his cancer?"

"Yeah tragic. Is he going to be alright?

"He says he is. But I don't know Steve."

"We should do the freak tribute thing."

"No way you stupid crazy Nazi boy," I said straight back. No hesitation. Not doing that. Steve had other ideas.

"Yeah, Baz used to love that. I know he was only the roadie but he thought he was part of a right laugh. If you can still call me Nazi, then we can still do the freak thing."

'No Freakshow' was the weirdest, most surreal thing I'd been involved with. Bell had been away one weekend to visit an old rugby playing mate at another university. Bangor in Wales I think. He'd watched some band called 'Freakshow'. Bell said there were 300 people there but he says he's got nine inches. I've seen him in the shower. It wasn't a cold day. *More Chipolata than Cumberland.*

When Bell came back from the university in Wales, still comatosed by alcohol, he suggested we should have a tribute band to Freakshow – a tribute band to a band no one's heard of? Of course. Being such a stupid and wacky bizarre idea, we all agreed.

You'd think Bell, having his hands up other men's backsides in the scrum, would be ideal for the drums but he was self-appointed lead singer. He could break a glass with that voice. Then swallow the glass fragments destroying his vocal chords further (do not try that at home). And why have one singer, when two would sound even worse? Chinny was also lead singer. Joint lead singers. It hardly worked for Fleetwood Mac and it most definitely didn't work for us.

Steve S (Nazi) was on drums. He had no idea what he was doing but he looked the part. Baz was the roadie carrying equipment in and out. I was given the role of manager – I was seeing a local girl called Sue Dann (she was English but with her 'African' name being half-way between Chad and Ethiopia, it helped my Kofi Annan nickname keep going). Her dad was distantly related to a bloke whose next-door neighbour had a friend who knew someone else who owned a string of bars in the city so that got us enough

275

gigs. Nine gigs in fact. The latter six cancelled after they heard about the first three but it gave Baz some lifting of cymbals, microphones and a keyboard to do. Oh yes, keyboard, that was Khan.

Well, he played the electric guitar, the triangle, the bass guitar, the saxophone, the trumpet and an accordion – all by pressing a few buttons on his £2,000 state of the art keyboard. He could do drums on it too and often did to drown out Steve's murdering beats but we never told Steve that.

"Look over there," Steve persisted. "I spotted it as soon as I came in. Full band gear at the back of the stage."

There were electric guitars, a bass guitar, trombones, saxophones and a trumpet. Perfect set up for a professional ska group. We didn't need all that. We'd had enough *red red wine*. All we needed were two mikes, a set of bongos (which Steve was happy with) and a keyboard which was leaning up against the wall.

Khan, Bell and Chinny didn't need much persuasion. Drinking alcohol between breakfast and now helped. Baz was overjoyed. As they were setting up, he tapped the mike....

"One   two   one two." He can't actually count to three. "Thank you all for coming to the Baked Bean Bash. Baz's *baked bean bash.* Yeah, I like that." A couple of cheers and hoots.

"Get on with it," shouted Gold.

"Big thanks to Mr Flinch for letting us in here. His good wife-to-be for giving me a hand gel." Baz was pleased he'd said 'gel' and not 'job' with Gold looking on. "She hasn't stopped serving us drinks and big thanks to the huge, hench henchmen. So many others to thank......

Ziv for letting us smash up her car.

Mr Thrush for driving us. His hareem for filling the dancefloor early on.

Our Chinese friends for defending us against a bunch of school kids.

Alexa, wherever she is, for the music.

Kate for bringing Steve.

Bapsie, Badger, the paramedics, the police and....."

Baz stopped talking and pointed at a man emerging out of the darkness.

"....the Lithuanian van driver.......what you doing here? Wow. Yeah, thanks for picking us up all those hours ago and not driving over us in your search for fuel. There's a beer for you at the bar.

Thanks to the *Bake That* bus women for dancing to everything non-stop. You've worn off all those cake calories." They cheered, shouted and a few even flashed their tits.

"But most of all......

Big thanks to Animal, to Lee and to my crazy five mates behind. I love the lot of you.

It's not been easy lately, but enough of that. Let me introduce to you, a tribute band with a difference.

'*NO FREAKSHOW*' - a tribute band to a band that shouldn't be tributed   if that's a real word, as they're not even famous.....

.

Ladies and gentlemen   and Badger over there.

I give you:

No Freakshow."

Khan hit the first key of his saxophone, trombone and instrument ensemble with perfect timing. Bell and Chinny were poised on the microphones. Lee was filming and Steve had his hands in a cross of drumsticks above his head........

He makes political decisions

Regarding hospitals and prisons,

But he never seems to satisfy his wife.....

All he does, he does, he does for you,

He could turn the sky from grey to blue,

But he never seems to satisfy his wife.....

Everything seems right....

....till they switch out the lighttttttt

Yeah yeah yeah yeah yeah

She's using a vibe tonight

She's using a vibe tonight

She's using a vibe tonight

A vibe tonight

A vibe tonight

The crowd loved it.

The *No Freakshow* tribute act that can't be a tribute band returned with a few other unknown unchartered and uncharted 'hits' such as '*Entercourse*', '*Drinking*' and '*Smooth Talker*' before giving everyone '*Vibe*' one more time.

The chorus was being screamed out by 'The Vibettes' – the Bake That fans who were close to changing group allegiance (Bros, Kajagoogoo, Aha and Right Said Fred had all now slipped down the boy band league table). Steve grabbed a large full-length mirror from behind the side curtain and reflected it off Baz's beaming face - Baz King was now on stage, albeit it via the mirror.

At the very end, Chinny and Bell took turns to thank the audience – this being the main problem with having two lead singers. The Gallagher brothers struggled with power almost as much as Chinny and Bell but at least only one person in Oasis sang.

I walked from the side of the stage over to Baz who was looking on proudly from the very rear of the room. He had one single tear in his eye.

"I've just recorded that live on my phone," he said with emotion in his shaking voice." I nodded knowing no words were needed. "Might be the last time   I hear that. Last time   we're all together. I had to record it." That same tear was meandering a way down Baz's face.

"Nah," I barely managed to say.

He scrolled across to what he'd saved it as. "Listed it as....... '*The boys (No Freakshow)*'. Then I put '*Vibe*' see? She's using a vibe tonight.   Yeah. Classic. I could have saved it as '*Sophie's song'* yeah?" he said. "I bet she's using one right now, eh?"

The tear dropped to the floor.

24

Baz walked to the exit unaided though my arm around his shoulder would have helped. His body was thinking less than his mind. His head was crying less than his eyes. His heart wasn't broken but it was more than dented.

He feared what was ahead for him. Or what wasn't.

Gold stopped us. "There's more beer behind the bar lads. It's all gotta go."

"I'll have some of that," Bell declared.

Bell had only just returned to nuzzling into the headteacher – she's probably not a headteacher. Maybe she's got a better job like a shelf stacker at *Asda* or toilet cleaner at *The Mollynogging* public house – very few jobs can be worse than a headteacher, suffocated by hundreds of snotty kids and having to go to a school every weekday of your life. Sunday evenings used to be torture as a kid. Once *Bullseye* had finished, it was just waiting for the next day, sitting by inkwells, in front of blackboards, carrying text-book bricks and being weighed down by a blazer that you never ever did grow into. Ji-young grew into her blazer. No wonder sitting behind her lifted up my day.........and lifted up one other thing.

Teachers do get long holidays but they still com-plain about clocking off at 3.30pm. And those big metal fences outside every school......they're not to keep the terrorists out, they're to keep the teachers in. Still, easy job I reckon but I wouldn't want to do it. Bell's got a lot of kids. Five minutes looking after them is worse than herding cats.

One thing is for sure, if she is a headteacher, Bell will enjoy her redundant six whacks of the cane at home.

Each day starts with pleasure and then gets better. Today was different. It improved quicker.

Lee was already outside beaming. He had two bot-tles clunking together in his left hand.

"You drinking Lee?" I asked, surprised.

"Yep, I'm starting as you lot are finishing. Cheers everybody. It is gonna be a long journey back otherwise."

He'd set his camera up on a wall with a couple of beer mats tilting it up at an angle.

"I'm going to show the highlights of the day projected up onto the side of the club. My camera automatically picks out the best bits at random and then I can play all our *Lads Reunited* malarkey back."

Baz and myself were at the doors ready to thank all who exit. I felt like I should have been in a white wedding dress and Baz in a top hat. We were stood either side of the doors. Khan was first to see the fresh air.

"Anyone seen Alexa? Where the bloody hell is she?"

"I saw her get something off Basil Thrush about one hour ago and then last seen chatting to one of the henchmen."

"Fuck," said Khan. "This is why I brought her. Stop her going down that greasy path again."

Baz didn't help the situation: "You don't think she's shagging one of the henchmen do you   in the back of the library?"

"No, I don't.   In fact, I definitely don't. The henchmen are on the wall over there and she's   well, her focus is elsewhere."

"You mean she's a lez?"

"No, I bloody don't mean that. She's,   well,   had difficulties with online gambling and loot boxes in games. Not good. Wiped away a lot of cash. I thought she was over it. Anyway, why am I sodding talking about it?"

He ran to the library. Concern for his daughter was clear.

Bell came out next with his arm around the headteacher. He looked hungry for his short-skirted new love and hungrier for large fat fried chips.

"You've just missed it guys," Bell said proudly grinning. "I've just asked Jasmine to marry me and she said yes." He showed us the chewing gum wrapped around her finger. "Gold doesn't sell *hula-hoops.*"

"You serious?"

Bell looked at Jasmine. Jasmine looked at Bell. A blissoming "Yes," they both bleated with sexual desire. Her top was a little dishevelled and unbuttoned. I noticed the word, 'Jason' beneath her left breast was smudged. True love.

"Buy a ring first thing tomorrow Bell?" Baz asked.

"No mate, priority tomorrow is getting some cheap flights."

"You taking Jasmine somewhere hot?"

Bell looked surprised. "Hot? No Baz, I need some cheap flights for a darts match Monday night."

The police, paramedics, Uncle Rog (yes, he turned up just as it was all finishing) and the remainder of the Bake

287

That gang, including the drivers, all left shaking our hands and thanking Baz. Frankie slipped a piece of paper into my hand. I didn't look at it. It went in my back pocket.

Bapsie and Badger stumbled out.

"You're welcome at *the Mollynogging* anytime you are passing boys. Just phone to let us know you're visiting in case we're busy. Badger will do his speciality onion soup."

"Thanks Bapsie," we said. We'd skip the soup. We've seen the remains of it in the base of a toilet pan.

Chinny and Ziv came out hand in hand.

"We're not getting married. We're not having sex. We're just holding hands because if one of us falls over, the other one can pick them up."

"You're getting the QP for that Chinster," an incoming voice beamed towards us from within the exiting crowd. Four people partitioning the *Bake Thatters* and heading directly at Chinny. A mirage surely.

"Kurgan. Jenkins," Chinny cried out.

Jenkins looked exactly the same as he had done 27 years ago. Maybe even younger. Peter Pan.

Kurgan looked like he'd enjoyed many a full monty full English fully loaded breakfast for 27 years. Frying Pan.

Kurgan held aloft two trophies. Two females followed.

"They were in my attic," – the trophies, not the females (I assume). Jenkins and Kurgan embraced Chinny first, then the rest of us. Sonya (from environmental science and still looking like Sonia Fowler) and Hannah (from geology, still looking like Anna Friel and still visibly able to hang clothes off her nipples) stepped forward. We've no idea who was with who. It didn't matter. Jenkins and Kurgan, both teachers with the highest level of privacy, camouflaged on social media and hidden from modern view since the website '*Friends Reunited*' went into digital abyss, were back with us.

"Jenkins, Kurgan," Steve Stevenson whooped.

"Bloody hell, Nazi boy," Kurgan responded. His attention drawn towards Gwyneth 'Kate' Paltrow and whether she was more QP than Ziv – we didn't normally have a decision to make over who got the QP cheerleader trophy. Us lot bagging a QP came along as often as a reunion bus. Steve, Kurgs and Jenks all showed each other 27 years of love.

"Oh Baz," Steve said. "We meant to say, Kate and me are expecting a baby. We've known for a few months but we've just agreed.   We're going to call it 'Baz' after you."

Before Baz could reply, Basil Thrush came by carried by Tonka, Dumper, WL and The Bin (Dusty finally had a nickname). Skinny Latte was holding his stick (his walking stick that is) and BJ was carrying his teeth. "That's lubbly name furz your babby. Sozzy, not speaksing properleez, Brahms and Liszt," Basil Thrush said with increasing difficulty. He winked at Baz. "Now, there's three of us," he said.

"Make that four," said Animal.

"You having a baby son as well Animal?" Baz asked.

"No, not a son."

"You having a daughter and calling   her Barry?" I asked hesitating.

"No, I'm going to adopt a *cabbage patch kid* and get the name of him changed to Baz. My wife collects them."

There were two questions to be asked. Both had equal rights to being question number one as both questions needed clarification from the double shock we'd just heard. I asked them both as one question:

"You're married and you're getting a cabbage patch doll??"

"Whooooaaaaa. Please! *Cabbage Patch Kid.* Don't call the little people dolls. And yes, I am married. She doesn't look like Gwyneth Paltrow, Anna Friel or Nicola Cassidy   or any celebrity   because she is a celebrity."

Animal is alive. Shock.

Animal is married. Shocked.

Animal is adopting a doll, sorry toy....kid. Shocking.

Animal is married to a celeb. Hold the front page.

Animal panned his phone around 180 degrees, sliding pics of him and his celebrity wife.

I was beyond words and beyond thoughts. I felt as if I'd consumed a dozen *Slush puppies* ice cold and my brain wasn't defrosting.

Khan came back with Alexa. Both looked ok with each other.

Baz nudged Khan and whispered, "I hope she hasn't put any money on us getting back before 8am."

Khan was less discreet with his reply: "No, nothing like that Baz. Very proud to say Alexa's been on the library revising for her A levels   and she's 18 now."

We all congratulated her on her birthday.

"But...." Khan added, "....bad news is she tells me she wants to do literature at the same uni we all went to." Khan was clearly relieved, proud, shocked, still hungover. He sat on the wall just behind us. We all joined him. Khan took off his prosthetic legs. "These are aching," Khan said.

"At least you're not in high heel women drag shoes," Baz replied.

Jasmine, still drooling over the back of Bell, looked down. She didn't twitch at the sight of Baz wearing sparkly heels but said to Khan, "I didn't realise you had no legs."

Bell replied for Khan, ".....and he doesn't know you've definitely got legs – he just gets on with life. Khan's a piss head to be honest. Always legless, even when he's not been drinking."

"Right," Lee shouted over. "The highlights are ready." We were all grouped together on the wall – Baz King's Men. "Alexa, can you play Oasis ' *Wonderwall* ' over the top of my highlights and I'll press play."

We all looked up to where it was about to be projected. Next to me:

Baz, Imran, Bell, Lee, Ed.

Gold came out and sat down. He was one of us now. Everyone else was behind. They're all part of us.

"Whooooaaa. Press pause," Baz shouted. "Where's the Chinese six?"

They came out of the club with perfect timing. Baz gave each of them a hug. "I can't speak Chinese, Cantonese, Mandarin, whatever you guys speak but I loved having you with us."

"We wery appy to be here Baz," their karate kid said, stopping short of kowtowing Baz – we called the kung-fu fighter Jerome after the patron saint of libraries – Lee had researched it all (without being asked) online.

"So, you're going to like disappear into the English cities now? Go under the radar or claim refugee status? I'm interested," Baz asked.

"No, no, no, we at university study English liture and we on weekend wisit to Shakespeare birthplice. Stratford-Upon-Avon. Now Stratford-Upon-Coventry."

"But you were in the back of that van hiding, being people smuggled?"

"Yeah, yeah.   So were you Baz. You refugee too?" They all started laughing. Baz joined in. We all did. Baz put his hands up kung-fu style to extend the joke. We didn't.

"We onlee in van because our bus not pick us up. Apparentlee bus compannnie send me email. Look here. It say that some idiot call Barry cancel two buses and book them for Sunday instead. They not give me monies back."

"Bloody idiot," Baz said. "Right, sit yourself down. Lee, press play."

Me greeting Lee,

Baz pointing at my shirt of spunk (toothpaste),

Chinny morphsuited up and opening Thelma and Louise,

Khan and Alexa arriving by taxi,

Bell skidding in,

Bell showing us his knickers,

Baz pacing round on the
phone,

Us all getting in the
Lithuanian van,

Baz ordering his *happy meal*,

Us almost getting run over,

Lee crashing the car,

Baz hiking into marshland and then storming into a
painted war zone,

  Basil arriving,

    finding the mobile library,

      picking up the bingo girls,

action footage in slo-motion of the martial arts
versus skateboarder battle,

  Chinny resurfacing,

    Bell throwing a mobile phone,

      Badger coming out the
      toilets,

Bapsie behind the library speeding on her motorbike sidecar,

    Baz coming back on the library holding a
    dented tin of baked beans aloft,

      the police photos,

killing Animal,

      arriving at the closed club,

            Gold unlocking the doors,

                  Baz trying on heeled shoes,

the Bake Thatters flashing their tits,

        music, dancing (sometimes coordinated)

              BJ with her husband's heel lodged
              between her cheeks,

Nazi arriving,

      the Vibe chorus,

              Kurgs and Jenks arriving trophies in
              hand

                 and

Baz shaking hands with everyone.

"Brilliant. Thank you all. Let's go home," Baz said. For the first time in his adult life, a BJ was the last thing Baz needed now. But Berol interrupted, pointing at her husband and saying, "He's no use. No way he can drive us all home."

Several thoughts went through my head.

Room on the *Bake That* bus?

Calling Frankie?   *Travelodge*?

Sophie nagging me for getting home late?

Changing the fish water?

Sleeping on the floor of a sticky soon to be demolished club floor?

Waving the white flag and just giving up?

For once, no one had any answers.

"I'll do it," a gruff chiselled voice came from within the pack. Rising up out of the ashes was the Lithuanian van driver. "I'll do it. I will drive you all back."

"Thanks Mr   Lithuanian driver man."

"Well, I have run out of petrol in the van so I need to get home somehow."

Baz's Road Trip Reunion Celebration thing:

Signed, sealed, delivered. ☑

Lads Reunited. ☑

<u>Reasons to Celebrate</u>......

☑University Reunion

☑Road Trip

☑~~Stag Party~~ Having a new baby

☑Driving Test ~~celebration~~

☑50th birthday   ☑Thelma & Louise empty

☑New job   ☑ 18th birthday

☑Just here for the beer.....and getting married

☑Weekend trip in the UK x6

☑'New' van for the Lithuanian ☑ Divorce Party

☑Belated retirement party ☑Jackpot win on the bingo x6

☑Bapsie has some customers ☑Badger gets off the loo

☑Animal finds religion ☑Club ready for demolition

☑Police photo with a hero ☑Paramedics save old couple

☑Uncle Rog finishes work for the night

☑QP and KM trophies re-discovered

☑Bake That event booked for next year

Most people slept on the way home. We dropped the Chinese off in Stratford-Upon-Avon. Steve and Kate directed them to a budget hotel just down the road from their five-star luxury pad. The Nazi and Paltrow hadn't upgraded to the family room with a cot......yet.

Badger and Bapsie said they'd take in Ziv for the weekend and help her sort stuff out. Bapsie said she'd had experience of it all before and knew how to help. Uncle Rog picked her up after the weekend (he had more jobs to do – apparently two buses full of *Take That* fans broke down on the M1 going north – he's got two weeks supply of cakes to get through now).

Mr Thrush and his menagerie of women (who were all truly beautiful on the inside and the outside) lightened the load when we dropped them all back at Basil's. Mr Thrush and six women but only two spare rooms so I'm sure he had a busy Sunday. I never understand why women go on diets and try to get thin. You ask any man what he finds attractive and most will say curves and big bottoms. And vice versa. All these men down the gym and most women love 'love handles' and a bald head. No wonder

Bell does so well. Bell and Jasmine (you realise she'll become Jasmine Rice – a long grained variety) stopped in Coventry. Got a room. We'll see her next in six months at their wedding. We'll see him next in *KFC* tomorrow night.

Kurgan, Jenkins, Sonya and Hannah went back to their hotel. Jenks is competing in the city triathlon tomorrow. Kurgan is watching. He kept the trophies. It wouldn't have been fair to rob them off him 27 years on. Afterall, he went back to the hotel with Sonya and Hannah. Trophy wise, that's doing the cup double again.

If Kurgs could work his magic with the hotel receptionist who apparently looks like Gail Platt from *Coronation Street*, then he could take the high road and have his own soapy soap opera triathlon.......or at least try. If, by absolute chance, *See-through Simon* is in the room next door, let's hope the curtains are opaque.

Approaching the giant roundabout of the south, the M25, Baz woke me up.

"This is for you," he said. "I've got one for everyone." Early morning light was piercing my eyes.

"What is it?" I asked. I was surrounded by books and he was passing me another.

"I brought them with me. It's my book. I've written it."

I held the book firmly in my hand. I didn't want it to slip away. I gripped Baz on the shoulder with my other hand.

"Wow," I said, my eye lids flickering, comprehending what this was, "you've written your own book?"

I took my hand away from his shoulder. I didn't want to but I needed to open the cover, gliding my hand over the words. '*By Baz King*,' it stated.

This was really his book. I jumped into the first page:

'And so it ends. I will die. No more stories. No more life. One last fight. This is my story before the end comes.'

"It's a life story. My life story. Kind of biographical but fiction too." I was lost for words. Baz was struggling but he had a few he's practiced a few times before today: "I'm giving it to you now as I've just read the email from the hospital. I went for an update last week but asked them not to tell me." There were tears welling up in his eyes. "I said email it to me and I'll read it Sunday morning. I didn't want any news spoiling this weekend."

"And what does the email say?" I asked tentatively.

"Yeah, all good news," he said, wiping his eyes. "My last petals might be trembling on the stem but good news. All the results are clear."

I paused. Hesitated. I knew Baz well. Well enough. I didn't want to say anymore because 'all the results are clear' was language I wanted to accept even if it wasn't true. I'd accept that. But I couldn't.

"That's not what it says is it?" I asked returning my hand to his shoulder.

Baz paused. Just nodded. "No," he barely said with his bottom lip gripping his top one.

"*My Life Before The Fight*, by Baz King. Can you sign it Baz?"

"Nah," he said wiping his face with his sleeve. "I'll sign it this time next year. We'll do this reunion again next year. I'll be here, don't worry."

There wasn't much of the journey left but Baz went round the library, waking each one of the others up in turn. Each person: Chinny, Lee and Khan played out the same emotions and body language as I had. We were all mirrored in our sadness but none of us wanted to show too much of it to Baz.

The van driver dropped us off. Clear light of day. Khan gave him some money and his number on a card. Khan said he'd be able to find him a job locally. No idea what happened to the library. I'd like to think it was taken back, the bus was fixed and the van was re-fuelled, picked up but more than likely, Chinny has the mobile library in his back yard and he's got his wardrobe of fancy dress outfits hanging up in it. Hopefully the books are still in there and someone has painted over the squirrel's log.

We hugged each other, slapped each other on the back. Alexa took a photo of us and posted it on fb as 'The Survivors'. Bell commented on it straight away and sent us all a photo in private messenger of him and Jasmine kissing up close, tongues out and named it, 'The Salivas'.

The morning air was smiling. Even the grass is singing I thought. The leaves in the trees were almost dancing. 24 hours ago, I was waking up slowly and now I'm approaching the road I live, with a blood bounding boyish feeling.

I followed the breadcrumbs and soon got back to the house. A brave new world. The light was on upstairs. All seems well. Sophie must have given herself nightmares, woken up and be reading aloud in bed. She's probably on page five by now of '*The Talented Mr Ripley*'. She's got a steady reading speed of about four words a minute.

I walked into the bedroom. There was a note on the bed:

'*I've had enough. I've decided to leave you. I've packed my bags and gone. Bye.*'

I immediately picked up the phone.

"Heather?   Hi Heather. She's gone.   Yes, Sophie's left me. Can you believe it?   I'm coming straight over to yours. Put on that little skimpy lingerie thing I bought you. I love that.   I'll be filling you up in no time.   Ok, that sounds good. See you in five minutes."

I walked out of the room but waited the other side of the door. I heard Sophie move, an internal growl fizzing out of her. Her stomping feet told me she was furious and her grizzly breathing portrayed shock, tension, hurt. Ready to explode.

She read the note that I'd left her (written when I was 'on the phone').

'Hi Sophie. I saw your feet sticking out under the curtains hiding.

I'll make us two teas and I'll be back up. I've missed you and I love you.'

She opened the door and we kissed. We actually kissed.

"That *Chopper* T-shirt is shit," she said.

Acknowledgements:

"Right, sit yourself down. Lee, press play."

Thanks to my son for inspiring me to write.

Thanks to my family – all of them. My parents: always unbelievably supportive (I even had a *Big Trak*, an *Atari 2600*, a vinyl Grease soundtrack, a Chopper, a Fonz action figure, a Corgi Blakes 7 ship, Shoot annuals, a *Casio* keyboard and a set of *Weebles*).

Thanks to Keith, MLO and Charles for reading the first draft and offering incredibly useful feedback.

Thanks to Kurgan, Jase & Jenks – the original Freakshow band who are now a band that ARE tributed (that's not even a word)! Original lyrics enclosed with appreciation and cameo appearances gratefully received.

Thanks to pixabay and pxhere for images.

Thanks for so many stories and to so many storytellers (factual and fiction; family, friends and famous) that have filled my mind and nudged my insides...........and.....

........thanks to everyone that has shared a drink with me over the years, some of which have offered the occasional idea for something in this book. Far too many ideas to fill one book and far too many people for me to remember but here's a few: Lim Tong, Duncan Wardrobe, Danny Hop, Idris Henley, Usher, Denham, Scotty, Jason, Aled, Wrigs, Eelco, Vealey, Maaaartin, Si and Jon, Lee, Bruv, Ronnie, Richard the Scar, LaLa and _____ (leave gap for people I have missed out to write their own name in).

"You'll all be in it. Bit of you in that character. Bit of you in this character. Bit extra from Bell's imagination and then the character evolves and adds a bit themselves. But I'll change the names."

24 chapters, 24 hours, 24 amazing books

"I can not declare my vows to just one book."

The following books are just 24 that I would whole-heartedly recommend:

1. The Talented Mr Ripley by Patricia Highsmith

2. 1984 by George Orwell

3. Harry Potter and the Philosopher's Stone by J.K. Rowling

4. The Great Gatsby by F. Scott Fitzgerald

5. Breakfast of Champions by Kurt Vonnegut

6. Restoration by Bell Rice

7. Metamorphosis by Franz Kafka

8. Eleanor Oliphant is Completely Fine by Gail Honeyman

9. Pride and Prejudice by Jane Austin

10. The Invisible Man by H.G. Wells

11. Brighton Rock by Graham Greene

12. The Crow Road by Iain Banks

13. Hand In Glove by Michael Ross

   Far From The Madding Crowd by Thomas Hardy

14. The Tattooist of Auschwitz by Heather Morris

15. Fear and Loathing in Las Vegas by Hunter S. Thompson

16. Five Children and It by E. Nesbit

17. 20,000 Leagues Under The Sea by Jules Verne

18. A Certain Slant of Light by Laura Whitcomb

19. A Tale of Two Cities by Charles Dickens

20. Captain Corelli's Mandolin by Louis de Berniéres

21. American Psycho by Bret Easton Ellis

22. The Curious Incident of the Dog in the Night-time by Mark Haddon

23. A Room of One's Own by Virginia Woolf

24. Lads Reunited by Max Speed

   My Life Before the Fight by Baz King

I often feel as if I am swimming through novels, pausing to dance on particular pages.

The video had gone viral. 27,000 views before we were back on the road

Contact Max Speed

He / she would love to hear from you. Take 1 minute & send an email

Email: maxspeedauthor@yahoo.com

No mention on *Wikipedia* yet

☑ **Do you want to appear in the sequel?**

– contact *Max Speed* by email and you may be chosen to be in it.

☑ **Get book 2, the sequel, *'Lads Reincarnated'* before anyone else.**

– contact *Max Speed* by email and you'll hear about it first.

Lee on the other hand, with all his diagnoses, ailments and mystery illnesses is National Health Service. Lee's been so much, he **reviews** it on *Trip Advisor*.

Thank you for reading *Lads Reunited*, my debut novel (yes, a novel as it's just over 40,000 words). It didn't quite take 27 years to write but I really would appreciate you taking 2.7 minutes to write a review on *Amazon* (not *Trip Advisor*).

Many thanks again and keep reading,

Max Speed

Printed in Great Britain
by Amazon